THE NORTHMAN'S LULLABY
AN ANDROMEDA'S ACCOUNT NOVELLA

L.B. BENSON

EMERALD MOON
PRESS

ALSO BY L.B. BENSON

ANDROMEDA'S ACCOUNT

The Bartered Soul
The City of New Aphros
Andromeda's Vengeance
The Northman's Lullaby

THE WOLVES OF WOODBINE HOLLOW

Sunset Daydreams
Neon Elegies

THE NORTHMAN'S LULLABY
AN ANDROMEDA'S ACCOUNT NOVELLA

By
L.B. Benson

First print edition February 2024

Cover design by Hampton Lamoureaux / TS95 Studios www. ts95studios.com

Edited by Kelly Hammond
Pickles Publishing

ISBNs
979-8-9861231-9-6 (eBook)
979-8-9896350-0-9 (Paperback)

Published by Emerald Moon Press
https://lbtheauthor.com

CONTENT WARNING & AUTHOR'S NOTE

The Northman's Lullaby is an adult fantasy/romance that contains content that might be upsetting for some readers. It is intended for readers over the age of 18.

To view detailed content/trigger warnings, please visit the author's website: https://lbtheauthor.com or scan the QR code below.

Important — Please Note: While *The Northman's Lullaby* is set before the events of *The Bartered Soul,* it *does* contain content that WILL SPOIL *The Bartered Soul.* Do not read this novella until you have read at least Book 1 in the *Andromeda's Account* series, if not the entire trilogy.

For anyone who's counting down the minutes, months, or miles until they see their love again.

xo, LB

CHAPTER I
ERIK

Approximately Five Years Before the Events of The Bartered Soul

"Bil—" I catch myself before amending my words. "Captain! Over here," I call down the street to my friend, who was only recently named captain on the ship we both call home — the *Bartered Soul.*

We have quietly followed some of the bastards who fancy themselves soldiers in King Dargan Blackwell's army, waiting for them to give any sign as to what they search so earnestly for in the streets and alleyways of the port city of Athene. Too busy pushing their way through the towns-people going about their day to notice us trailing behind, the three men already turned the corner toward the residential portion of the town. But in the darkened alley to my right, the slightest movement caught my eye, and muffled coughing made me pause. Now, I wait between the two buildings for Captain Lennox to catch up to me. As I lean against the brick wall, arms crossed over my chest, I squint into the gloom. The soldiers had glanced down the alley, I saw them over the heads of the few people I traveled behind, but they kept walking, clearly missing the glimmer of copper tucked in the darkened corner.

Lennox's golden hair reflects the watery sunlight streaming through the low cloud cover as he confidently strides down the street. The hard slant to his lips and the sharp cutlass at his belt make the townspeople wary, but I know the man beneath the façade. He and I have been like brothers since he joined the pirates of Captain Jackson's *Selkie's Tears*. Lennox sailed with us for nearly a year, growing to be like a son to Jackson. He moved up the ranks swiftly, and when he earned enough coin and notoriety to take his own ship, he named me his quartermaster.

Lennox and I work well together. His brash cockiness — a front to disguise his turmoil over the loss of his family to Blackwell's invasion — is balanced by my quiet calm. The men love Lennox. Respect him. Follow him as their captain with very little pushback. But they know *I* enforce his rules.

I learned early in manhood that a six-and-a-half-foot tall Northman does not have to speak loudly to be heeded. It has been just shy of six months since we began sailing with our own crew, but I know it will not take long for rumors of our reputation to spread throughout the ports of Selennia and across the sea.

"Why did you stop following them?" Lennox asks, his voice a low rasp as he reaches my side, eyes traveling over a pair of women walking to the market. Even as he waits for my answer, he offers the women a sly wink and lascivious smile. They dip their heads to mask the blush on their cheeks, and scurry past us trying to avoid more of our attention, their smiles hidden behind their hands as they whisper to one another.

I answer with a jerk of my chin toward the back of the gloomy alley. Lennox cocks his head to the side as he inspects the trembling bundle I indicated, then cuts his eyes upward to me with a frown.

"Did you see who it is?"

"No," I reply. I am fairly certain the figure hiding beneath the rags is a woman, but I did not see her slip through the streets to know for sure. I have no idea if she is who the men seek, but something, perhaps the voice of the Goddess, told me I needed to stop and look here.

"Well, why don't we find out, shall we?" Lennox murmurs.

We both look around for any patrols, but all we find are townspeople who quickly avert their eyes and cross the street. No one wishes to be involved with us, or whatever business we may be conducting, in the secluded alley. Stepping into the dimness, Lennox pauses to slip a small blade from his boot into his palm, then continues into the narrow space. I follow behind, watching the alley entrance, my axes within easy reach.

As we near the trembling bundle of fabric, I realize it is a wool blanket pulled tight around the small figure. The copper glint I spied from the entrance of the alley is still visible — a small section of hair that has slipped free of the blanket in whatever haste they used to try to hide. Our boots crunch on the grit of the cobbles beneath them, damp with discarded nightsoil and other detritus of city life, and as we approach, the pale, freckled fingers clutching the blanket whiten as they grip the threadbare fabric.

"Well, we've found you — you can loosen your grip on the blanket before you hurt yourself," Lennox scoffs. I cut my eyes toward him, pressing my lips together at his brusque tone. The hands are either those of a woman or a child, no threat to either of us, but until he determines who is beneath the fabric, I know he will not soften. At his words the fingers loosen, a shuddering sob escaping the blanket, followed by another round of coughing. The wool drops to reveal fiery red waves surrounding the creamy freckled face of a young woman.

"Well, hello there," Lennox murmurs, beginning to crouch down to inspect her. But as she raises her glassy blue eyes to look at us, Lennox sucks in a breath as though he has been punched. There on her brow is a fading crescent sigil, branding her as a former priestess of the Goddess.

CHAPTER 2
SIOBHAN

My fear is a living thing coiled in my chest as the footsteps approach, almost burning as hot as the fever raging through me. I thought I'd finally escaped the soldiers when they allowed me to visit the apothecary shop alone once we reached Athene. I should have known they wouldn't let me get away that easily. My value as a healer for their troops outweighed the order to destroy my kind, but I don't think they'll be merciful if they find me.

The fever I contracted forced the physician to whom I was bound to allow me to replenish my supplies and seek a remedy to soothe the illness burning through me since none of his methods had offered relief. As soon as the apothecary ushered me out the back door, I ran as fast as I could in my weakened condition — without proper shoes, decent clothing, or any idea where I was running to. The elderly man had given me a wool blanket from the back room as a cloak of sorts to hide under as best as I could. For the first time in my life, I was angry that I had inherited my mother's shining red hair, even as lank and greasy as it is now.

Upon hearing murmurs of soldiers tracking a woman, I dashed down the alley, thinking I'd be safely hidden amongst the trash and debris of the city. But here I am, huddled in a blanket with nothing to defend myself with beyond a package of antipyretic herbs. I try to control the shaking in my limbs and the nagging cough that aches to be released from my throat, aggravated by both the noxious smells of the close alley and the illness that grips me. Tears well in my eyes as I look up at my trackers, but instead of the soldiers who escorted me through the town earlier, I find two unfamiliar male faces staring down at me.

One is strikingly handsome, his golden hair shining even in the dim light I cower in. My eyes drift between him and the tall man looming behind him who wears his dark hair in the style of the Northern Isles. Neither of them wears uniforms that identify their allegiance to Blackwell or otherwise, offering me a sliver of relief even as my headache throbs and my vision blurs from my illness.

"Priestess," the blond murmurs as he begins to crouch near me. Involuntarily, I shrink back, pressing myself against the wall as if I have any way to escape. Even if these men aren't part of the army, the mark I bear is still a beacon for danger. They may very well turn me over to the ones I flee from, or worse.

"You don't need to fear us. Let us help you." His voice rumbles again. Although the alley is dim, light glints on the small blade he holds in his hand. When my eyes land on it he looks abashed and sheaths it in his boot before looking at me expectantly.

"Captain—" the Northman starts, drawing both of our attention.

"You there! What are you doing?" a shout comes from the mouth of the alley and the Northman turns quickly to guard the other man's back.

"They found me," my voice cracks in my burning throat, and I begin to cough again.

The cough is deep and racking which sends pain through the muscles of my ribcage and abdomen, forcing me to brace my arms around my torso for any relief. Tears blur my already hazy vision, both from my cough and my fear, but I can still make out the three soldiers who seek me standing backlit in the mouth of the alley. I'm not sure if they can see me, burrowed in the blanket, but I cringe anyway knowing they'll have heard me. I'll face punishment for this, even if they wish to keep me alive for my healing skills. I've learned I can still work after meeting the lash or the cane, bruises don't slow one for long.

"They may have found you, but they will not have you," a lilting voice states through the gloom. I realize the lyrical sound comes from the towering Northman who now wields an axe. The accent is one that brings me comfort and, even though I shouldn't, I find that a glimmer of hope blooms in my chest.

I sink back as far as I can when the blond unsheathes a cutlass from his hip and moves to stand next to his tall companion. Side by side they almost fill the narrow space, but I worry about them fighting two against three.

"Can we help you?" the one the Northman called *Captain* sneers, a surprisingly vicious smile tugging at his lips.

"We're searching for a redheaded witch. You wouldn't happen to have found her, would you?"

"Witches are for children's stories; I wouldn't think grown men such as yourselves would be troubled with them."

"If you know what's good for you, you'll both get the fuck out of the way or else you'll meet the king's justice," another soldier chimes in, stepping forward with his hand on the hilt of his sword.

A cold laugh bursts from the captain. "I don't think the bastard on the throne knows the definition of justice. And I don't think he should count on cowards who believe in bedtime stories to enforce it."

"You son of a—" The insult is cut short with a gurgle and a cry.

Pulling the blanket tight around me, I peek out just in time to track the Northman's empty hand reaching behind him to pull a second short-axe from where it was strapped to his back. The other must be... I risk moving slightly to see between the men's legs and find the missing axe lodged in one of the soldiers' chests where he lies choking on blood in the muck of the alley. The other two soldiers have drawn their swords, stepping past their dying companion without a second glance, and approach the two men who block their passage to me.

A dark laugh escapes the captain as his blade sings. He easily parries against one of Blackwell's men, while the Northman takes advantage of his sheer size and evident strength to disarm the other, hacking into him with the axe. My eyes dart between them, a mixture of fear, nausea, and relief all warring in my fever-weakened body. At least the two strangers will keep me from going back to the camp.

When they first came upon me, I feared they might try

to ransom me to the king's men, but if that were the case, they would have just handed me over or negotiated a trade here in the alley. I'm too exhausted to worry about what other motives they may have for taking me for themselves.

As the soldier fighting the Northman falls, my focus turns back to the captain, whirling and parrying in his dark greatcoat. A wild grin slashes across his face as he easily avoids the soldier's blade. It's almost as if he's enjoying the fight and toys with the man like a cat does its prey. After a few moments, I realize that is exactly what he's doing. Each time he avoids a blow he slides his blade across the other man, in places that injure but don't incapacitate. As the soldier falters, the captain's grin seems to glow brighter, and his feral eyes catch the light when he turns toward my direction.

Finally, the soldier stumbles and falls to a knee in the damp alley. Somehow, we've avoided notice thus far, but I know it's only a matter of time before someone peeks down the row to see what's happening, although the sheer brutality of the men who fill the space might keep the pedestrians' eyes facing forward instead of taking note. Before I can worry over the thought more, the blond man sheaths his cutlass, pulling the knife from his boot once more. He maneuvers so the soldier now faces me directly while kneeling in blood and filth.

"Is this the *witch* you seek?" the blond growls.

I shudder as fear eclipses me, wondering why he would reveal me now.

"You're going to pay for this when they catch you, whore," the soldier spits toward me.

"No. She won't," the captain says, grabbing a fistful of

the soldier's hair, and yanking his head backward to look up into those savage eyes as he whispers, "But you will."

Then, without further warning, he drags the sharp knife across the soldier's throat, spilling a wave of dark blood down the front of his uniform. All I can think of as the man is pushed to the ground is how lovely the crimson of his blood looks against the black cobbles of the alley, and how well his once tidy uniform now matches the ugliness of our surroundings.

CHAPTER 3
ERIK

I keep an eye on the woman pressed against the wall while I pull my axes from the men, wiping the blades on a cloth I ripped from one of their uniforms. I managed to avoid the majority of the splatter and do not wish to draw attention to us as we make our way back to the ship by being soaked in gore. It will be hard enough to avoid notice with a ragged priestess with us.

Her light eyes are still locked on the man at Lennox's feet, leaking blood into the mire of the alley. I cannot tell if it is fear, shock, or the overall trauma she has endured that keeps her motionless, but I replace my blades in their holders before approaching to avoid frightening her further. Lennox breathes heavily, his eyes glazed over after the fight. I clear my throat as I step forward to alert him of my presence. I made the mistake once of surprising him after a battle and was rewarded with a blade thrust in my direction. He blinks, the frenzy clearing and posture relaxing as he sheaths his knife.

"Priestess, would you like to get the fuck out of here

now?" Lennox asks roughly, looking over his shoulder toward the street beyond.

The woman still sits motionless, staring at the dead eyes of the soldier, as if she did not hear him. Lennox takes several strides forward, stepping over the lifeless figure, heedless of the blood he walks through, and crouches before her, his dark coat billowing around him.

"Mistress?" he questions, cocking his head. When she still fails to respond he looks over his shoulder at me, then reaches out slowly as if to touch her. At that, she starts, fear flooding her freckled face as she pushes the blanket off and scrambles sideways.

"Whoa! You're all right, we won't hurt you. They aren't going to take you." Lennox stands and steps back quickly to avoid frightening her further, holding his hands up as he reaches my side. "Maybe you should try, Erik?"

"Me? You think a giant who looks like a northern raider will put her at ease?" I whisper back.

She seems so small without the blanket covering her, kneeling in her threadbare dress and worn-out boots. Her copper hair hangs in dirty clumps over her shoulders and around her pretty face. Wide blue eyes dart between us, but she remains silent. The sigil at her brow, marking her as one of the women from the fallen coastal temples, is a dull scar instead of the bright crescent it once was.

"We need her to come with us and get the fuck out of here. You know the patrols will be around soon and she certainly won't want to be left in their hands. At least we can get her away from here, either back up to Celeste or over to Marie or Salome." He gestures with a sweep of his hand toward her as if inviting me to speak to the woman.

"I'm not going to grab her and have her kicking and screaming down the streets."

Sighing, I take a few tentative steps forward before crouching down to be remotely level with her eyeline.

"Mistress? Are you able to walk?" I ask softly.

The priestess' eyes meet mine and I barely manage to stifle a small gasp as her beauty fully impacts me. This close, her eyes are even more brilliant, and her creamy cheeks are dusted with copious freckles like stars in the night sky. Lighter streaks form a path of tears cutting through the dirt on her cheeks. Despite the cool air of Athene, she is flushed with a sheen of sweat covering her. As she looks at me, her trembling slows and stops, her breathing slowing to its normal rhythm.

"I'm not sure, but I think so," she hoarsely replies, a heavy brogue accenting her words.

"My name is Erik Varangr. Captain Lennox and I will not harm you. I swear to the Goddess Herself. Please, allow us to help you."

The woman furrows her brow slightly at my vow but does not flinch away when I reach my hand toward her to offer assistance to stand, her gaze tracking my every motion. To my surprise, she places her small palm in mine and allows me to pull her to her feet.

"Mistress—" I start to ask her name, but when I grasp her hand in mine, I realize how much warmer it feels than my own. Her skin is hot and clammy, almost painfully so. "You're burning up with fever!"

"Aye... yes, yes, I am. It might be that this fever is what has saved me... or what ends me," she says, swaying slightly until she leans her heated form against my side, struggling to hold in another round of coughing. She is so much smaller than I am, her head barely coming to the level of my chest, and I do not know whether to put my arm around her or just let her use me to prop herself up.

"*Erik!*" Lennox hisses while I try to decide what to do with my hands. "We need to go, now."

"Erik?" The soft rasp next to me pulls my attention down to her. My name on her lips makes my heart skip a beat for a moment. It has been a while since a woman said it so softly. "I... I think I might need you to help me if we are to move with any haste."

"Of course, Mistress," I answer and scoop her easily into my arms where she feels like a small bonfire held to my chest. "Captain, we are ready."

"Hold on. Let's not draw more attention than you already do," Lennox mutters, grabbing the blanket and wrapping it around the woman, only leaving a small opening for her to breathe easily. To her credit, this time she does not fidget or pull away from the man she just watched slit someone's throat. "Now perhaps they'll think you're just carrying provisions and they'll be too afraid of our weapons to bother us. Try to keep that cough quiet, Priestess."

"Are you all right, Mistress?" I ask before stepping into the fading daylight to head toward the docks.

"Siobhan."

"What?"

"Siobhan. You don't have to call me 'mistress'. My name is Siobhan," she murmurs against me before relaxing and allowing me to carry her through the streets.

CHAPTER 4
SIOBHAN

Despite my fevered condition, I clutch the wool blanket around me, seeking warmth from it while relishing the heat seeping from the tall man — *Erik*, I remind myself — who carries me like a sack of supplies through the streets of Athene. I shiver as chills rack my body and snuggle closer, hoping I can keep from coughing all over him. The other man, Captain Lennox, covered my face with the blanket and I have no desire to peek at the fate that awaits me. At this point, I don't think these men could be any worse than being forced to travel with and tend to the soldiers who destroyed my home and my sisters.

It takes little time to reach the docks with Erik and his captain's long strides. Through the moth-eaten fabric of the blanket, I hear the calls of sailors and gulls as the sound of Erik and Lennox's footsteps change from crunching on grit and cobblestones to the hollow clacking of boot heels on wood. The ocean lapping against the ships at anchor is subtle under the sound of the city, growing louder as their footsteps continue down the dock. When it feels like we are ascending, I allow myself a peek out of the blanket to be greeted by the side of a ship as I'm carried up a gangplank and onto the deck.

"What is it you've got there, Erik?" a deep voice booms across the way, and I scramble to pull the cover back over me. Despite the friendly tone, I'm unsure if my presence will be welcomed on the ship.

"Take her to my cabin, Erik," Lennox murmurs close at our side. "Give her one of my shirts if she'll take it. I'll have one of the cabin boys bring her some water to wash with."

"She's burning with fever, Captain." Erik's accented voice rumbles against my cheek.

"Water." My voice cracks from under the blanket. I clear my throat and move the blanket from in front of my face before continuing, "I need boiling water. Please. I purchased herbs to help with my illness in town. I need to steep them."

"I'll tell them to bring a kettle too, then," Lennox answers.

Hurried footsteps and shouts to get the ship underway surround us as Erik carries me to what I assume are the captain's quarters. The cabin door opens and closes quickly and Erik sets me on my feet near a dining table, bracing me as I wobble like a fawn. He unwraps the blanket from me far more delicately than I would expect such an imposing man to manage, then pulls out one of the wooden chairs, guiding me to it and indicating I should sit.

I practically collapse onto the hard chair, the effort of fleeing through the town and lack of nourishment catching up with my fever-weakened muscles. Once I'm seated, Erik scans me, as though expecting me to keel over. Apparently satisfied I'll remain upright, he crosses the room and opens a trunk near the bed. Shivering although my skin feels like it's on fire, I watch through the ropes of my dirty hair as he crouches by the trunk, the lean muscles of his arms and back contracting with his motions. He rifles through it as if the items are his belongings, not his captain's, before pulling out a long-sleeved linen shirt. Even though my head still aches, and the light from the large back windows hurts my eyes, I take in my rescuer as he returns to me. Some, especially those from the more refined towns, might find his appearance brutal to the eye, but I let my gaze drift over the designs inked on the shaved sides of his scalp and admire the bits of gold he's woven into his long braid.

Unlike his captain, Erik has dark facial hair covering his upper lip, cheeks, and chin, which hides his expression from me, but his blue eyes hold no malice when they meet mine. Despite his fearsome exterior, I feel no fear of this stranger and relax against the hard back of the wooden chair as he places the shirt on the table.

"What will the captain do with me?" I ask softly, fighting back a cough as my hands tremble at the possibilities.

"Do with you?" Erik asks, tilting his head as his blue gaze examines me.

"Am I to be his woman? Or…" I trail off, looking at my hands where they rest in my lap. My time spent in the army camp had been easier than other women's. I don't know why they chose to keep me as a healer and not as a whore, but I still thank the Goddess for it. I was lucky that the camp physician found me and claimed me instead of one of the regular soldiers.

"No. Lennox is not like that. No one will touch you aboard this ship, Siobhan." The serious tone is startling, and when I look up at him his features look like they're carved in stone. "We may be pirates, but we do not condone that behavior from our crew."

Pirates? I hadn't realized they were outlaws, but sifting through the haze of fear in the alley I should have. The confrontation with the soldiers would never have happened if these men weren't outside the law. Most others would have cowered and backed down at the soldiers' commands, turning me over to them to do as they pleased.

Despite my rescue, logic tells me I should be more frightened than I am. But between the aches and chills from my fever, and the exhaustion resurfacing now that my panic from the fight in the alley has subsided, I find that I'm not fearful. At least not of Erik. I've been frightened for so long that I'm now only tired and relieved.

"You're from the north, I take it?" I question, but Erik's response is cut short as I begin to cough in earnest. I hug my arms around my ribs to stave off the pain as best as I can.

"I am, but we can discuss that later if you wish. How can I help you? What do you need?" he asks, kneeling at my side, one hand hovering as though he would pat my back or soothe me in some way before he thinks better of it.

"Water," I manage. He grabs a pitcher from a desk and pours water into the first glass at hand, something far more suited to brandy or other liquor, but I drink gratefully nonetheless.

As the coughing subsides and I catch my breath, a knock at the door draws our attention. Erik strides across the room to retrieve a bucket of water with soap and a cloth, as well as a kettle with steam rising from it. Placing them on the table in front of me, he looks at me expectantly.

"The herbs? What do I need to do?" he asks when I furrow my brow.

"Oh. Yes, of course."

I shake my head, my vision is beginning to blur as the fever rages, but I pull the packet from my pocket and unwrap several smaller parcels with my shaking fingers, each one labeled in the elderly apothecary's handwriting. For a moment my heart stumbles thinking about the kind man, hoping the soldiers haven't harmed him, but then how would they have known he assisted me? And now that they're dead, it doesn't matter anyway.

I separate a small piece of ginger, cradling the valuable root gently, then sort the packet of dried elderflowers, dried peppermint, and the small vial of honey I was able to procure. Erik quickly takes them from me, chopping the ginger with a knife from his belt, then dumping in the measurements I advise. As the mixture begins to steep, the spicy aromas of the ginger and cooling peppermint soothe me, filling the unfamiliar cabin with comforting scents. Finished with his task, Erik steps away from the table, clearing his throat once to draw my eye. I notice he always moves as if I'm a creature that might flutter away, an injured bird or some other delicate thing, making sure I hear him before he speaks and that I know where he stands before he moves to avoid startling me.

"While you wash and change, I will see if I can obtain more suitable garments for you. Until then, Lennox's shirt will have to do," he explains, holding out the linen shirt once more. "I will come back, or send a cabin boy to check on you. We must get underway."

I'm not sure where they would obtain women's clothing on a pirate ship, but then who knows what spoils they might have stashed away from raiding one merchant vessel or another.

"Thank you, Erik," I answer after clearing my throat and offering a weak smile. Perhaps it's the fever or a figment of my imagination, but I swear his cheeks flushed when I said his name.

"Do you need anything else before I leave?"

"No."

He gives a quick dip of his chin in farewell and retreats from the cabin. With the door closed tightly between me and the crew of pirates, I breathe a shuddering sigh of relief, then wring out the cloth to wash the grime from the alley and the army camp away. Cleansed as best as I can, I sloppily braid my hair, then wrap my hands around the warm mug to wait for the tea to finish steeping. I say a soft prayer to the Goddess, asking that the herbs will relieve the ache in my head and muscles, and ease my burning fever. And to thank Her for this respite at last.

CHAPTER 5
ERIK

No answer greets me when I tap at the door of the captain's cabin after we reach the open sea. Luckily, our crew was on board waiting for Lennox and me to arrive, so we were able to set sail without delay or scrutiny from the harbormasters. We paid them handsomely to look the other way upon our arrival. I do not think anyone aboard would be happy to part with any additional coin from our shared spoils to avoid nosy soldiers. Not to mention a tall blond man and a dark-haired Northman would be fairly easy to identify should anyone remember us from the area near the alley. Much better for us to leave immediately.

After no response from my second knock, I open the door quietly, peeking in to check on the priestess. I had the cook heat some broth for her and brought it with a pitcher of cool fresh water to help her with her illness, balancing the two in one hand as I push the door open completely. Siobhan still sits at the table where I left her, but instead of wearing her tattered dress, she is clean and dressed in only Lennox's long shirt. Her red hair is braided in a thick plait, although some strands hang loose as though she tidied it in a hurry and missed a section, and she rests her head on her arm on the tabletop next to a mug.

My eyes drift briefly over the creamy, freckled skin of her legs, bared by the short hem of Lennox's shirt, before anger surges through me. Bruises and scrapes mar her knees, likely from whatever ordeal she endured at the hands of the soldiers, and her bare feet have raw marks from ill-fitting shoes.

"Siobhan?" I whisper. I do not wish to alarm her, but I also do not think Lennox intended for her to sleep at his dining table. "Siobhan…" I brush a hand against her cheek, pulling it back hastily when she stirs. But she does not wake, just knits her brow and continues to sleep. This close I can see her shivering. I gently touch her forehead, feeling again for fever, and am appalled at how hot she burns. The tea is partially consumed, but even though I do not know this woman, I worry about the heat radiating from her. I also briefly worry for the men aboard the ship should her condition spread easily, a fever could ruin us in the middle of the six- to eight-week trip to Delosia or New Aphros.

The third time she does not respond, I carefully scoop her up and carry her to Lennox's bed, tucking her under his coverlet. He will have to either sleep with the crew, or on the spare bed in my cabin until we figure out a destination for her. For some reason, the idea of him sleeping in the bed *with* her is not one I even consider. He would not harm her, but the idea of her curled up next to my friend chafes. I shake my head at my thoughts. I know nothing about this woman aside from the fact that she is pretty and currently unwell. It has been too long since I have had the pleasure of female companionship if I am daydreaming about a stranger.

Siobhan whimpers softly once she is in bed, her brow again furrowing at whatever haunts her sleep. I think back to when I still lived in my village, to when my siblings or I were ill, trying to remember what our mother had done to care for us. Flashes of her pressing cool cloths to our foreheads, while she hummed lullabies, come to mind. So, feeling foolish, I mimic the action with a bit of the cool water from the pitcher and one of the cloths I brought for washing.

The lullaby comes back to me easily, even after all these years, and I hum the melody softly while I attempt to bring down Siobhan's fever. Soon, the lines between her brows ease and she seems to fall into a peaceful rest. I should leave the room, leave her to heal with the water and broth on the table for her to drink when she wakes. But, for a few minutes, I simply sit in a chair at her bedside, my elbows resting on my knees with a cool cloth hanging from my hand as I watch her sleep.

WHEN THE CABIN DOOR SWINGS OPEN, I STAND QUICKLY FROM the bedside chair I still occupy. Lennox strides into his cabin, looking around for the woman, but stops in the middle of the room when he finds her in his bed, sleeping soundly.

"What are you doing, Erik?" he whispers, not

approaching further. I make my way to the desk across the room, gesturing with a wave for him to join me near the windows at the stern of the ship so we do not disturb Siobhan.

"She is ill, Billy," I inform him, keeping my voice low.

"I assumed as much with that cough, but I can smell herbs." He inhales deeply as though seeking the source of the scent. "Did she take something for it?"

"She drank the tea she made, but was already asleep when I came back in to check on her."

"Rather presumptuous of her to take a nap in the captain's bed, don't you think? What if I took that to be an offer?" Lennox chuckles softly, giving a smirk and raising his brows. His smile fades when he looks up at me, the brash façade replaced with curiosity. "Erik? Are you all right?"

Realizing I must have been glaring, I give myself a small shake, then explain, "*I* placed her in your bed. I told her you would not harm her, but she was sleeping at the table when I came back in. I was unable to rouse her, so I moved her to be more comfortable. It is clear she needs the rest to heal."

"Mmm hmm." Lennox purses his lips and hums. "Erik Varangr, do you fancy our fiery-haired priestess?"

"Do not be ridiculous. I do not know the woman. I am treating her with the same care I did the others we have found. This one is just ill and exhausted and needs a bit more attention." I protest but feel my cheeks redden at the lengthy explanation.

"A lonely man doesn't need to know a beautiful woman

to want to be near her, Erik. And you, my friend, are a goner."

I know he believes in the truth of his words and that he is not just being a cocky bastard. He himself pines over a woman he only met for a night, looking for her at each port, even having the figurehead of his ship carved in her likeness.

"Give this one some time before you start questioning her, Billy. She needs the rest."

As if punctuating my statement, Siobhan begins coughing in earnest, tossing in her sleep as she does so. We both turn toward the small figure in the bed as she settles back to sleep, making sure she is not listening to us, before Lennox answers.

"I'll give her time; we'll have plenty of it on the way to Delosia. Let's just hope she bought enough supplies to get rid of that sickness before anyone else catches it. I'll let you know if you're needed on deck, in the meantime feel free to watch over your woman." He winks at me standing there with my mouth open, wanting to contradict his statement, then laughs once, lays his discarded coat across the back of a chair, and exits before I can think of anything to say.

"Erik?" a small voice calls from the bed as Siobhan sits up, rubbing sleep from tired eyes.

"Yes?" I reply, hoping the dim cabin light hides the blush rising to my cheeks at hearing my name on her lips.

"I thought I heard men's voices. I wasn't sure if any of it was real or if I was back in the tents."

"You will not go back there, Siobhan. Drink this and rest."

I carry water, broth, and cold tea to her, offering them each in turn as I sit by her side, ignoring Lennox's words and the warmth growing in my chest when I catch her glancing at me from the side of her eye.

CHAPTER 6
SIOBHAN

Several days pass while I recover from the worst of my illness. Surprisingly, Captain Lennox hasn't removed me from the comfort of his cabin, remaining noticeably absent from his quarters. Erik has made certain to refill the pot of hot water and steeps the herbs as I instructed, providing a constant stream of broth, water, and herbal tea. Even though I no longer suffer from a fever, the cough, headache, and malaise persist, making me dip in and out of poor sleep throughout the days while my muscles ache.

One cloudless morning, I wake squinting in the bright light from the back windows, to find Erik's tall frame stretched out on the soft, exotic rug, sleeping soundly as if he's a guard dog keeping me safe. He has one arm overhead, acting as a pillow while the other rests across his stomach. His still booted feet are crossed at the ankle and he has no blanket to cover him, almost as though he was simply keeping watch and dozed off. I hadn't realized he spent so much time in the cabin while I recovered. He's always been in motion, coming and going throughout the days when I did wake. Embarrassment warms my cheeks, both from wondering what he's been doing here the whole time and because I desperately need to relieve myself and don't want him to catch me when he wakes.

Squirming under the blankets, I look closer at my surroundings. An assortment of books and parchment are stacked on Lennox's desk near the windows that line the back wall, while another small stack of novels rests on the table next to the bed. Mismatched chairs are tucked under the dining table where two lamps await a lit reed to illuminate them this evening. When my eyes drift back over the rug in the center of the floor, and the man lying on it, I run my eyes over his lean physique, admiring his long legs, trim hips, and broad shoulders. As my attention travels higher, a startled gasp escapes my lips when I find clear blue eyes returning my stare. I cough from the quick intake of air and hope he will think it was the cough that caused my reaction in the first place.

"Good morning," he says softly, sitting up and resting his forearms on his bent knees.

"Good morning. What are you doing on the floor?" I ask before realizing that the alternative would be sharing the bed with me.

"Lennox took my berth while you occupy his cabin. I hope you do not mind me sleeping here."

"Oh. I see. No, I don't suppose I mind. It's only…"

I don't know why I'm embarrassed to tell him I need to relieve myself. I spent enough time in the camp with the soldiers to have been thoroughly relieved of any modesty when it comes to bodily functions around men, even if I would rather not think about that. I pointedly look over to the chamber pot and Erik's eyes widen.

"Of course. Excuse me, I must have slept later than I realized." He unfolds himself from the floor, stretching as he moves toward the door. The white linen shirt he wears is identical to the one he wore when he found me in the alley, but I don't know if it's the same one he wore then, or if it's a staple of his. Either way, it stretches tight across his broad shoulders as he walks away from me, and I almost have to drag my eyes away from him against my will when he opens to door. "I will bring some food for you shortly. You seem to be feeling better?" he questions, silhouetted by the door.

"I am. Still tired. And sore. But overall, much better. Thank you."

"That is good. Perhaps later you would like to walk on the deck to get some fresh air. You are free to do so whenever you wish." With a dip of his chin, he steps from the cabin, and the door clicks shut against the growing sunlight.

ONCE I'VE SEEN TO MY NEEDS, WASHING IN THE BASIN OF water that was left for my ablutions, I wonder when my breakfast will arrive and if they were able to find me a clean garment. Erik's offer for me to walk on deck sounds refreshing, but I can't stroll around in front of a crew of pirates in nothing but their captain's shirt. It hadn't crossed my mind to bring it up when he still reclined on the carpet.

As I sit at the dining table gazing into a mug of tea, my

eyes become unfocused, the edges darkening as my vision narrows on the liquid in my cup. For a moment, panic sets in and my heart races as my head swims. I felt better when I woke up, how is it that I'm now on the verge of fainting?

Struggling to calm my nerves and slow my breathing, I realize this isn't my illness. It's now such an unfamiliar feeling that I barely recognize that I'm being granted a vision until my sight begins to distort more. It's been a long time since a vision has come to me unbidden; since I've felt a connection to the Goddess without my sister priestesses at my side. Tears line my eyes and my pulse begins to race anew as my breaths become shallow and uneven with excitement. Unblinking, I stare at the surface of the tea while the crescent symbol of the Goddess floats to the top. It's framed with blackness — hair perhaps? Am I seeing a woman? A priestess?

My visions are never certain, never clear pictures or stories, and never easy to interpret. But the hair on my neck rises as I continue to focus on the liquid. I never know how long I succumb to the *Sight,* but when I finally blink my eyes, I nearly leap sideways.

Erik kneels at my side, braced as though he worries I might topple over, his eyes intent on my face as he angles toward me. His silence is startling for such a large man, but then, I was so keen on seeing more from the vision that I can't be sure I would have heard him either way.

"You are a *Seer,* then?" he asks, sitting back on his heels for a moment before he stands, drawing my eyes upward. I'm momentarily distracted by his sinewy forearms as he crosses his arms over his chest, but I quickly look away from them and into his eyes.

"What do you know of *Seers*?"

"We had one in the village where I grew up. She was connected to the Goddess, like you priestesses. Some things might be different, we might have more myths, but our beliefs are not so dissimilar."

I already knew that the people who live on the Northern Isles worship similarly to how we once did in Selennia, how I still do in my heart. When I first showed signs of being talented with divination I delved further into their legends, but I'm hesitant to share too much with this stranger. Even though he has been kind and gentle, I have to remind myself that he and his captain murdered three men without seeming to think twice just a few days ago. It *was* only a few days, right?

"What day is it? Where are we sailing?" I ask, my voice still raspy from my persistent cough.

"We sail for Delosia. It has been nearly five days since we departed Athene."

"Delosia? Across the ocean?" my voice trembles. I've heard of the island across the sea but assumed these men were merely sailing to another Selennian port to drop me off.

"Yes. It is usually a six-week voyage. Athene was our last stop in Selennia. Lennox avoids the southern tip since it is where the navy is thickest. He did not think you would want to remain where the army could pick you up again. And you were in no state to protest otherwise. I am sorry if you are displeased with the destination."

"I'm not displeased," I whisper, allowing that faint glimmer of hope to bloom brighter in my breast. "I'm relieved."

I look up into his eyes after my confession to find his lips have twitched up into a smile in response.

CHAPTER 7
ERIK

Although I am surprised at the words Siobhan speaks, the relief that visibly washes over her makes me smile, and when her eyes meet mine my heart stutters in my chest. She gives a small smile in return before flicking her eyes back down to the mug of tea between her palms.

"Did you find any clothing for me? Besides the Captain's shirt?" she asks, still not meeting my gaze fully.

The reminder of her lack of clothing causes me to involuntarily glance again at her bare legs where they peek from under the table, but I avert my eyes quickly, hoping she did not notice the look. I am not some lecher trying to take advantage of a sick woman just because of her forced proximity, especially not one as gentle and shy as Siobhan seems. Although pirates have the reputation of taking whatever catches their eye, be it treasure, goods, or women, this ship is not run that way and this crew will not tolerate it. If any of them would, Lennox is certain to root them out and put an end to them.

Clearing my throat, I move toward the bundle of

clothing one of the crewmembers gave me when I asked for women's attire. I placed it on the bed as I walked by to speak with Siobhan, but she has not noticed it since blinking away her *Sight*.

"I did. They might not be a perfect fit, but they should make you more comfortable."

"Thank you, Erik," she replies, taking the bundle without looking up at me.

The sound of my name on her lips makes my breath come more shallow than normal, makes me want to caress her cheek to offer comfort, but I know I should let her dress and give her space. When I begin to pull my hand away and step back from the table, she lays her small palm on top of mine. The pale, freckled skin stands out against the weathered tan of my own and I freeze looking down at the contact, drawing my brows together. "Thank you for the clothing. But also, thank you for your kindness."

"Of course. I will allow you to dress." I start to pull away, her touch burning into me even though she no longer has a fever. She turns in her seat, still touching my hand as she looks up at me.

"I would like to walk on the deck after. I know you're likely busy, but..." She breaks eye contact and looks down at our hands, still touching. "But I was hoping you might show me around, just the first time?"

I barely breathe as sparks tickle along my hand where our skin touches, my belly clenching when she looks back up at me with her guileless eyes.

"Of course. Anything you wish."

If she only knew how much I mean those words.

I wait at the base of the stairs looking over the main deck, arms crossed over my chest, as the crew bustles to complete their tasks — manning the rigging, cleaning the deck, shouting to one another over the sea breeze. Lennox descends from the quarterdeck, where I assume he was discussing our course with the helmsman. Siobhan has not opened the cabin door yet, and I do not wish to crowd her, not after she found me sleeping in her room this morning, so I wait where I have a view of the door without standing directly outside it.

I did not mean to be present when she woke, but I succumbed to a deeper sleep than I expected after several nights of poor rest on the hard floor. I was not being dishonest by telling her that Lennox took my berth, but I also did not admit that there was another bed available in my small quarters that I could have used instead of sleeping on the floor in hers. The first night I stayed because I was concerned for her well-being, not wanting her condition to worsen without someone knowing. As her fever broke and she seemed to be feeling better, I worried she might be frightened should she wake alone in a strange place. But I have to face the fact that I also wanted to be the one she sought when she needed something, wanted to be near her.

As Lennox approaches, a smirk tugs the corner of his mouth up, his green eyes traveling between the door to his cabin and me.

I hate it when Lennox is right. I *do* fancy the woman, even if it is a purely physical reaction. I do not know enough about her to have true feelings for her. Even though I remain silent and expressionless, my friend's sarcastic expression turns into a full grin as he nears me.

"Good morning, Quartermaster," the Captain greets me, clapping me on the shoulder.

"Good morning, Captain."

"How is our guest faring today?" he asks, standing across the stairs with his arms crossed, mirroring my stance.

"She seems well. She asked to be shown about the decks to take some air."

"Wonderful, perhaps I can ask her my questions and take my cabin back then." Lennox's voice still teases, but I know he means what he says.

Curiosity glints behind his eyes. I suspect waiting to ask the priestess his questions has been eating at him. Based on his recent grumbling, I also know he would prefer to return to his quarters instead of my smaller cabin below deck. "I'm sure one of the crew can show her around, I need you to —"

"No." I interrupt.

"No?" He raises a brow at my tone, leaning against the rail of the stairs to look up slightly at me. "Varangr, need I remind you that you are my second on this ship and are still subject to my orders?"

"No, you do not need to remind me. But I will show her around. She is not fully well yet. We do not know how she might react to the crew, and I do not want to risk her safety. I am sure she will answer your questions afterward," I reply, adding, "Captain," to soften my defiance.

Lennox's eyes dance with amusement. We rarely disagree, but he says nothing more as the door to his cabin cracks open. Siobhan peeks from within, drawing both our gazes. She has her hair braided back from her face and wears the loose dress one of the crewmembers handed over at my request. The roughspun fabric is a deep russet tone, only a few shades darker than her hair, and offsets the bright blue of her eyes. Without meaning to, I worry that the coarse material is uncomfortable brushing against her delicate skin.

What is wrong *with you?* I wonder, pushing off the rail and taking the few stairs down to the deck.

Lennox follows, our boots stomping on the wood as we approach her.

"Good morning, Priestess," Lennox greets in a soft tone, much softer than I usually hear him speak, all teasing and brashness gone.

"Good morning, Captain," Siobhan replies in her soft brogue as she looks toward her feet. "Hello again, Erik," she directs to me, lifting her blue eyes to mine before looking away, her copper lashes fluttering to match my heartbeat.

"Varangr tells me you wish to walk the decks this morning. Afterward, I have some questions," Lennox states, cutting his eyes to me as if to challenge me to speak up again.

"Of course, Captain," she whispers.

"Siobhan," Lennox says, drawing her shy gaze. When she looks him full in the face he continues, "You have nothing to fear from me or my crew. Do not flinch from us. You're safe here. Do you understand?"

"Yes. Thank you, Captain."

"Are you ready?" I ask her.

"I am."

CHAPTER 8
SIOBHAN

Erik maintains a respectable distance from me as we stroll along the damp planks of the deck, walking me from stern to bow. The spindrift leaves little droplets of seawater in his long, dark braid as we walk, drawing my eyes even as I try to keep them focused on the ship, the sails, the ocean — anything besides his handsome profile. Most people in Selennia would shrink from a man who looks like one of the feared raiders who used to appear in the stories Selennians told their children, but the brutal exterior masks the kindness he's already shown me, and I find that I can't stop thinking about the familiar lullaby he hummed while I dozed the first day I was aboard.

I'm relieved that I have more strength and energy than I have in the weeks since my illness surfaced, far better than I would have expected if I was still trapped with the soldiers in their miserable camp. I'm fortunate that the physician insisted they stop to allow me to visit the apothecary, but I wonder if he had any idea he was offering me the chance to escape. I shake my head to dispel the memory of the man. I hope after a few more days I'll be fully recovered. The constant stream of broths and tea, along with being indoors and off of the cold, rough ground that was my bed for far too long, have made all the difference.

"You said you're from the north…" I start, gazing out at the waves, hoping to start a conversation.

"I am, yes. Some of my family still lives on the Northern Isles."

"But, not you? Why would you come to Selennia? Sail with a Selennian ship?" I prod.

"I come from a long line of sailors, as you can imagine. I took my chance at sea and ended up here." The gentle lilt of his accented common tongue brings a smile to my face, but his short answers, and my strained voice, keep me from rambling on to the laconic man.

When we reach the bow of the ship, I try to figure out the best way to once again break the silence, comfortable though it may be. As we rest our hands side by side on the rail overlooking the ocean, my eyes catch on the figurehead of the ship. Wrapped up as I was when I was carried aboard, I never saw the woman carved at the front of the ship. Now, I can't draw my eyes from the profile of a priestess with black hair curling around a painfully beautiful, masked face. One sapphire eye looks in my direction and my eyes settle on the silver, upturned crescent moon sigil of the Goddess peeking above the mask.

"Is the ship named for a priestess?" I ask, dragging my eyes from the woman to look up at Erik.

Erik turns so his back is to the ocean, resting against the

railing, elbows bent with his hands on either side of his hips. He glances down at me, then at the figurehead and back, before searching the crew for something. "It is a complicated tale, one that the captain is more equipped to explain. But, in some ways, yes. Perhaps he will share it with you when you speak later."

"I hope she brings you more luck than my sisters and I have found," I murmur, running my fingers over the fading sigil above my brow.

A lump of sorrow tightens in my throat as I remember the invasion by Dargan Blackwell's forces at the Northern Temple. The coppery scent of blood replaces the briny ocean, and the sounds of screams and steel in my mind drown out the crash of the waves. Our temple was the first to be attacked when Blackwell overthrew Queen Adelaide and took the land for his own. I watched as my High Priestess sacrificed herself, then hid until I thought I could safely try to heal any of my surviving sisters. When Black-well's soldiers found me, I was dragged away screaming, making myself just as hoarse as I am now. As each temple was taken, news of the suffering traveled to me where I was held captive in the army camp. I never heard the names of those lost. We were never thought of as anything more than pagan whores, why would any of the soldiers bother telling me which of my sisters were gone?

Instead, I was forced to assist the army physician to treat the wounds of those who deserved death in place of my sisters and the villagers who dared stand against the army. I still don't know why I wasn't killed outright like so many others, but the doctor, even if his tactics weren't always the kindest, made sure none of the men outright abused me. Tears burn behind my eyes, my throat tight with the heat of my anger, but wondering why I was spared won't bring any of them back now, and it won't ease the sadness I've nursed for years. I can't dwell on the past when a new future has been offered to me and my *Sight* is finally returning.

"Perhaps she has brought us all luck these past few days," Erik's lilting voice whispers, almost to himself, as he watches me closely. I dash away a stray tear that has escaped my lashes, and despite my memories, I can't hold back a smile as I meet his gaze, receiving one in kind from him before his cheeks flush. "Are you ready to speak with Captain Lennox now?"

Nodding my assent, we make our way back toward the great cabin. The crew surprises me as I watch them surreptitiously with sidelong looks. They seem tough and hardened to the elements, as expected, but a few of them are much younger and more delicate than the older men with whiskers and weather-beaten faces. Some of the younger ones even offer shy smiles with kind eyes, dipping their chins in respect to me as I pass.

"You and your crew aren't what I would expect for…"

"Pirates?" Erik offers.

"Sailors in general, but yes."

"I think you will find that Lennox is motivated differently than other pirates. His crew reflects that," he says when we reach the captain's door. His scarred knuckles tap on the wood before he opens it without waiting for a response.

Lennox sits at his desk, reclining back in his chair when we enter. He's shed the coat I've seen him wear since he found me in the alley, and is only clad in a worn linen shirt with the sleeves rolled up, paired with dark breeches tucked into broken-in boots. Tattoos swirl on his forearms, adding a formidable aura to the already intimidating man. Now that I'm feeling better, I take a moment to really look at the man who helped save me. Lennox is a man of paradoxes, his lips are full and sensual, completely at odds with his sharp cheekbones and the predatory gleam in his eyes. He reminds me of nothing so much as one of the mountain cats that roam the crags of northern Selennia.

"Welcome back, Siobhan," Lennox says, standing from the desk and approaching us. "I trust you enjoyed your walk along the deck?"

"Yes, Captain. Thank you," I reply, not meeting his eyes.

I can't shake the residual fear I have of Lennox, even though he hasn't offered any harm to me. Something about the wildness in his eyes when he killed the man in the alley haunts me. Although I know Erik was responsible for killing *two* men that day, I don't sense the same fury emanating from him. Nor did I get the sense he enjoyed the deaths.

Without thinking, I take a small step toward the large man at my side, and he tenses in response to the tiny movement. Lennox's dark green eyes dart between the two of us and his full lips lift into an easy grin.

"Erik can stay while we talk if you would prefer, Priestess. But I promise you, I mean you no harm."

"Oh!" I'm startled at the offer, but look up again to Erik,

hoping I don't seem as weak as I feel asking for his company. "Would you? I'm sure you have other duties to attend to."

"I wouldn't offer if I thought it would interfere with his duties," Lennox advises, approaching the dining table and pulling out one of the chairs.

"I will stay if you wish." Erik steps forward and pulls out a chair for me while folding his tall frame into the neighboring one. Taking a deep breath, I walk across the exotic carpet to the table and sit facing Lennox.

"Now, where do we begin?" Captain Lennox drawls, finally sitting and leaning back in his chair, arms crossed as he studies me.

***

LENNOX STARTS THE CONVERSATION EASILY ENOUGH. HE ASKS how I'm feeling, about my past, where I was born, when I became a priestess, what temple I lived in, and what skills I studied.

"I'm from a village far in the north of Selennia, several hours by wagon from Airmedan where I joined the temple at the Northern Point. I celebrated the rites at seventeen and lived there for three years as a new full-fledged priestess before the invasion. My main talent lies in divination, but I excelled in herblore and healing as well," I explain. "I suppose those skills, and the fact that I stayed behind trying to save my injured sisters, is how I ended up with the army in the first place." I don't like recalling when the soldiers came. I hid, locked in a secret pantry in our still room, while the main invasion raged, only escaping through the ravaged temple when the sounds of battle and destruction had faded.

"After I thought the men had passed through the temple, I snuck out and sought those who were wounded but hadn't yet perished. I was trying to heal one of my sisters when the army physician found me. I have no idea why he didn't turn me over for execution, but he insisted to the commanders that I be allowed to stay with him. He had a Selennian accent, not one of the continental ones like the other soldiers. Now, looking back, I wonder if he wasn't doing the best he could to protect me after all."

Lennox scoffs at my attempt at giving the physician any benefit of the doubt. "If he had wished to protect you, or any of those killed, he never would have sided with Black-well. I don't care if he was under threat of the sword or gallows. He was a fucking coward for siding with them," Lennox spits, his words cruel and contemptuous. Many have suffered at the hands of Blackwell and his army, but without him even telling me I sense Lennox has turned that suffering into rage and hatred.

"I can see your point, but then should the same be said for me? I did as they asked to survive," I challenge, shocked at my boldness in front of the captain. I don't feel any warmth for the man I shared a tent with for these past years, but I understand that sometimes one must do the unthinkable to survive.

"He may have been a coward and saved men who should have been left to rot, but I also know he saved me from being raped or murdered in that camp — allowing me to sleep on a quilt in his tent for safety without ever laying a hand on me. Even if I occasionally met the lash or the cane from the priests for disobedience, or for trying to call on the Goddess to help me heal a patient, the physician always stepped in. He always made sure to apply healing ointments to lessen the pain and damage."

Erik goes rigid at my side as I speak. "They beat you?" His accented voice sends a chill down my spine with its iciness. His large hands clench into fists on the table as he asks, and my stomach tightens at the sight of lean muscles coiled in his forearms.

Meeting his gaze, my voice is breathy as I respond, "They did, but luckily the scars are minimal. At least I still live."

"My scars are not minimal, Siobhan. I don't blame you for doing what you had to do to survive, I did the same. But we both escaped. That man remains complacent in his duties."

Returning my eyes to Captain Lennox, I add, "I think he helped me escape. If not for him insisting I go to the apothecary in Athene I would never have been allowed to slip away. I think in his own way he did all he could."

Lennox's lips tighten into a line, nostrils flaring as he considers my words, but I can't concentrate on his expression. Erik's gaze has rested on me since I admitted I bear scars from my time in the camp, his blue stare causing my breath to catch and my skin to heat under its intensity.

"So, you were only ever at the Northern Temple?" I nod, still focused on Erik. "Did you ever meet a priestess from the west?" A hint of desperation seeps into Lennox's voice and he sits forward, pulling my attention back to him. His hands are clasped on the scarred tabletop, and he's nearly begging as he adds, "Black hair, blue eyes, pale complexion? I think she would have been around your age." Lennox's eyes look fevered as he asks, hope bubbling behind the fierce gleam.

"I..." I turn over my thoughts, trying to remember if anyone passed through that bore that description. "I don't believe so. We had many who were dark-haired. Though none match that full description. Who are you seeking?"

"I don't know," he sighs, rubbing his palms over his face, then pushing his hair from his brow. "I don't know her name, or if she was even from the Western Temple for certain, only that I met her there... many years ago." Lennox's expression shutters, any hope fading from him. "Thank you for answering my questions, Siobhan. You may go now if you wish. I'll call on you if any others surface."

"Go?" I ask softly. I've been staying in his cabin since being brought aboard, I have no idea where else I would be going other than the room we sit in. I cut my eyes toward Erik, still sitting quietly at my side. His brow furrows minutely, but he remains silent as his captain speaks.

"Yes, you can take the spare bunk below. Now that you have recovered from your fever and are on the mend, it should be comfortable enough for you. I need my cabin back," he says, not unkindly. A sweep of his hand toward the desk reminds me that this isn't just his sleeping quarters, he uses it for business as well, and I have likely caused inconvenience to him these past days.

"Oh, of course."

"Erik, show her to her new room. Siobhan, we will speak again at another time."

Lennox dismisses us calmly, pushing back from the table to return to his desk without a backward glance.

I pause at the door, turning back to the captain. "Captain Lennox?" He meets my eye with hope. "I'm very sorry I don't have answers for you."

Lennox only gives a small dip of his chin in response, his jaw clenched tight, almost as though he doesn't trust his emotions to speak.

CHAPTER 9
ERIK

Siobhan stands from her seat and turns to make for the cabin door, red hair catching the light from the back windows as she moves, while my eyes shoot daggers at Lennox. When he sits at his desk he gives me a weak smirk, as though trying to hide his distress at her lack of knowledge. His resignation from her inability to answer his questions is only tempered by my discomfort at the new sleeping arrangement. When Siobhan stops to apologize for not offering more to help in his quest, I think for a moment that his emotions will betray him, but he keeps them tightly bound.

When I take Siobhan down to the cabin he described — *my* cabin — she will no doubt question why I have not slept in the second bed, instead of sleeping on the floor near her like a lonely puppy. The bastard knows he is forcing me to admit I have formed an unusual attachment to our guest. After this, I might be sleeping on the rug in Lennox's cabin for the rest of the voyage to Delosia.

I glare at my friend and captain once more, before

striding through the room to hold the door for her to exit. She walks quietly at my side as I head toward the stairs that will take us down into the hold, her eyes flicking up to my face occasionally, as if I do not notice the motion of her head tilting to look up at my height. I cannot tell if she looks at me with admiration or wariness since she always looks away so quickly, but my cheeks feel warm under her inspection regardless.

As foolish as I feel, I am unable to deny that I feel drawn to her. Not just because of her beauty, but because she has proven herself to be gentle and brave all in one conversation. The way she casually stood up to Lennox's challenge about the man who held her captive without flinching from him made me feel pride for her. She showed the goodness she still has in her heart, despite the things she has witnessed and experienced, even if her tale of being beaten by the priests made me want to return to Selennia to rip them apart in her honor.

Siobhan pauses at the top of the stairs, watching me from above with the sunlight framing her. "Are you all right?" I ask from the bottom of the wooden stairs. It is darker in the hold, but the lattice interspersed above allows some illumination to the stores.

"Yes, sorry."

She blinks a time or two, then quickly descends the stairs to continue following me. I point toward the stern of the ship, explaining where the rest of the crew sleeps, as well as to the cannons and stores held below the main deck. Turning to the right, we reach the door to the cabin, and I fight to keep myself from sighing too loudly. After hearing her story, I hope she does not think we are trying to trap her like the army did.

"This is where you will stay now," I say, pushing the door open.

The cabin is small, with two bunks, one on each side of the space, a plain table that folds down from the wall, a chair, and not much else. A trunk is tucked away in a corner, which holds my clothing, a small collection of personal effects, and weapons, but otherwise, the room is undecorated. A porthole offers light during the day, but several candles sit on the table for the evenings, and an empty hook waits for a lantern to be hung from it in the later hours.

"Whose room is this? I was under the impression the captain had been bunking with all the men?" Siobhan asks as she walks in to inspect the space.

"It is mine."

"Pardon?" she turns, looking up at me.

I clear my throat and say more loudly, "It is my cabin."

"I don't understand. I thought you didn't have a place to sleep comfortably while the captain stayed in your berth. But there are two beds here?"

"I was not comfortable leaving you alone," I admit, studying her face, and waiting for her reaction. "The other is for the boatswain usually, but Pike has always preferred a hammock so he stays in the main sleeping area with the men."

"Oh," she replies on an exhale. I watch as she swallows, her delicate throat bobbing before she worries her bottom lip with her teeth. "Where will you stay now?"

"I am sure I can find an extra hammock with the men to

give you privacy," I reply, turning on my heel toward the door to allow her time to settle in.

"You can stay here." The words are a soft exhale, barely audible over the creak of the hull.

Her words cause me to freeze, my back to her. My breath hitches in my chest for a moment as I blink, thinking I must have misheard her.

"Erik… You can stay here. There are two beds. I have shared a tent with a strange man for months, *years*. I'm not afraid to share this room with you now."

When I turn to face her, I find that she has stepped closer. Tension rolls off of me, my muscles trembling from the effort it takes to restrain myself from reaching out to stroke her cheek or her hair, or from taking her hand in mine.

"Do not compare me to one of the men who stood by and allowed you to be struck. No one will touch you while you are in my presence, Siobhan. Never. I promise you that." The words leave me more forcefully than I intended, but anger at the thought of her creamy skin bruised by a priest's cane makes my blood boil.

"What if…" she whispers, then pauses, taking a shallow breath and another step forward. When she looks up to meet my gaze her cheeks and chest are flushed, her words soft, as she says, "…what if I want *you* to touch me, Erik?"

My heart hammers in my chest at her words. Could I have heard her right? As if to answer my unspoken thoughts, she reaches out her hand to graze my fingers with her own. They linger on my skin, sending little shocks through me and making my stomach flip, while she looks up at me through her fiery lashes and the blush on her freckled cheeks deepens.

"Siobhan, you do not have to. I am capable of sharing this space without expecting anything in return."

"I know I don't. I understand if you don't wish for there to be anything physical between us, I just felt…"

Again, her words trail off as she moves to pull her touch from my hand as though embarrassed at her presumption. Before she can pull away, I grip her palm with mine, entwining our fingers as I bring her closer. When she is flush to my chest, so close I am certain she must be able to feel my heart galloping wildly, I tilt her chin up with my free hand to look into her face. Running my thumb over her flushed cheek I feel her tremble under my touch, but I am certain now that she does not do so from fear. Slowly, I move my hand so that it cradles the back of her neck, tangled in the red braid hanging down her back, offering her time to pull away from me as my eyes study hers. When I see she has no intention of breaking away from me I lean down and place a tender kiss on her mouth.

When I pull back, I whisper, "You see, Siobhan — I have felt the same."

Her lips curl at the sides at my confession, and then she grips my shirt in her free hand and pulls me back to her, pressing her mouth against mine. Our kisses deepen and I let go of her hand to cradle her face with both palms while she tugs me closer, using the fabric of my shirt to do so.

As our embrace becomes more urgent, lips parting and tongues exploring one another's mouths, Siobhan pulls me so we stumble to where her backside rests on the edge of the table, opening her knees so I stand between them. My cock aches with want for her, and each gasp and moan that drift from her throat as we kiss makes it harder to not press her for more.

"Erik," she breathes against my shoulder as I kiss down the column of her throat.

I pull away from her, breaking from her arms and stepping back. My breath is rough and uneven as I observe her, the roughspun dress hangs from one shoulder and the top of her pale breast rises above the neckline as she catches her breath. The temptation to pull it down to reveal her nipple threatens to drag me back to her. But she is still unwell, and I do not want her to do this out of a sense of obligation or gratitude for rescuing her.

"I want this, too," I murmur, taking a step back toward her and cupping her cheek. "But I do not think it would be right of me to do so while you are still recovering from your ordeal and your illness. I will gather your things from Lennox's cabin and bring them here with your dinner."

Losing my battle with my will, I stroke my fingers down her cheek, cupping her face for a moment. She turns to press a kiss against my palm and my chest tightens at the gentle touch.

"I'll be here when you come back," she says against my hand, then smiles up at me before I turn to leave.

CHAPTER 10
SIOBHAN

When the cabin door closes, I exhale deeply and scoot from the table I was sitting on, adjusting the neckline of the oversized dress so both shoulders are again covered. The deep breath causes my throat to tickle and my residual cough starts again, forcing me to sit on the bed to get a handle on my breathing.

Did I really just say that to him? Did that happen? I'm giddy, but embarrassed at my boldness. So unlike my usual self.

I, like most Selennian priestesses, am not troubled about propriety when it comes to bedding men. However, since my focus was divination and healing, I didn't participate in fertility or other rites that involved coupling with them as often as some of my sisters.

Even though we only met recently, something about Erik feels so safe and familiar that I couldn't bear the thought of him not sharing this room. It *is* his room after all, and there *are* two beds.

Not that I want him to sleep in the other one, I think, grinning like an idiot and touching my fingertips to my lips, swollen from our kisses. It's been so long since a man, or anyone for that matter, touched me kindly that I crave his gentle caresses and the feeling of his beard against my skin. These thoughts make me shiver as I curl on one of the bunks to rest, tired from our walk on deck and the memories kindled by Lennox's questions.

WHEN MY EYES OPEN, THE SUN HAS SET OUTSIDE THE PORTHOLE and a tray of food rests on the little table with a pitcher of water alongside a pot of herbs steeping. Somehow Erik, the giant that he is, was able to sneak into the room quietly enough to not wake me and leave these items, along with a low burning lantern and a pile of extra blankets which are stacked neatly on the empty bunk across from me. An extra dress and shift that he scrounged up from Goddess knows where also lays across the bed. Sipping the broth and the tea, I look out the porthole and watch the dark waves as we drift farther from my home.

I always wondered what life aboard a ship would be like. My grandfather told tales of life at sea from his younger days and shared legends of his and my mother's homeland as I grew up, blending the fantastic with reality. I delved deeper into the sagas at the temple since they had vast libraries full of texts from all corners of the world, but in recent years I thought my days would end in a dingy tent on hard ground.

Memories of my family, my home, my sister priestesses, and the dramatic changes my life has already seen bring tears to my eyes. I've spent so long trapped in an endless cycle of blood and death, commands and blows, that I didn't think I could still shed them. I assumed they had all dried out in the early weeks of my captivity. But, now — now, I have the chance to begin anew when we reach our destination, and perhaps in the meantime, I might have the opportunity to remind myself what it's like to seek comfort and pleasure in the arms of another.

As those thoughts rise to the forefront of my mind, the door creaks open, and Erik peeks in. I quickly rub my eyes, hoping the tears aren't obvious as I turn to greet him.

"What is wrong?" he asks immediately, stepping through the door to stand before me.

"Nothing. Just memories. I'll be fine."

I have to tilt my chin up to gaze into his eyes, my bare feet making me even smaller next to him so that I only reach the level of his broad chest. He hesitates a moment, his squinted eyes and knitted brow looking as though he's making a difficult decision. Then, he reaches for me and draws me against him, wrapping me in sinewy arms and his sea-soaked scent. Resting my cheek against his chest I breathe him in, relaxing and wrapping my arms around him, shocked at the ease with which we touch.

Has he been craving affection as badly as I have? Are we just two lonely souls in the right place at the right time? Questions stream through my mind as we hold one another in the center of the small cabin. Too soon, a small cough escapes, followed by another and Erik releases me to grab one of the cups from the desk to soothe my throat.

"Thank you. I'm fine, really," I whisper as I sip, trying to stave off any additional coughing.

"You should rest. What else can I get you?" he asks, clearly not believing that I really do feel fine aside from the lingering, hacking cough.

"This should all be fine. Are those blankets for me? Or you?" I change the subject looking at the stack of wool on his bunk with an arched brow. The man has been sleeping fully clothed on the floor of the great cabin, I'm fairly certain they're not for him.

"I wanted to be sure you were comfortable," he mutters, looking toward the blankets and then his boots with a hand gripping the back of his neck.

"You're very kind, Erik," I murmur, trying to come up with any reason to speak to him, to have him speak to me. A surge of pleasure warms my heart each time I notice his breathless reaction to me saying his name. "Have you ever..." I hesitate before speaking my thoughts, wondering if I'm being presumptuous or too bold again, but I steel myself and continue.

"Have you ever made a pallet on the floor here? Instead of leaving the mattress on the bunk?"

"What do you mean?" He looks thoroughly confused at my question, glancing between the beds.

"Well, if warmth is an issue, which you seem to think it might be judging by the number of blankets you brought in, I thought perhaps we could put both mattresses on the floor and, well...just sleep together?" My cheeks flush as the words rush from my lips. "Surely our body heat would be more warming than a stack of blankets?"

When I look up at him, he stares at me, eyes as wide as his grin. His lips are full, even surrounded by his facial hair, and his smile is slightly crooked, but right now it's one of the sweetest things I've ever seen.

"Well, I *have* been sleeping on the floor without a mattress since we departed Athene. I think it would be much more comfortable on one with you... if you are certain that will be comfortable for you."

My only response is a smile as I grip the edge of the thin tick mattress and yank it to the ground. He mimics my action with the other one once he moves the stack of blankets and extra dress to the vacated wood and rope bed frame. We tuck the two bed ticks close so there is no gap in between, allowing a narrow border around the edge for us to walk. I plop down on the side I've claimed for my own, pulling down several of the blankets to make a cozy nest. Satisfied, I sit in the middle drinking the remainder of my broth and tea and nibbling on a hard biscuit that accompanied my tray, perfectly content with the direction the evening is heading.

CHAPTER II
ERIK

The day is turning out to be very different than I envisioned when I woke on the floor of Lennox's cabin this morning.

The captain was all smirks when I resurfaced on the deck after showing Siobhan to the cabin.

"How did the change in quarters suit our guest, Varangr?" he asked, green eyes twinkling.

I could barely keep my hand from drifting to my lips, the memory of our shared moment still lingering there. In truth, it was harder to pull away and leave her sitting in my — *our* — cabin than I would have imagined. Although she has given subtle glances and has met my eyes more than a few times when they drifted in her direction over the last few days, I never expected her to welcome my touch. Let alone ask for it.

"She took it in stride, Captain," I replied, ignoring his narrowed gaze as he studied me.

"Hmmm… glad to hear it. Hopefully, things won't be too cramped for the rest of the voyage," he said feigning seriousness. "I still have some questions for her, but we have plenty of time before we get to Delosia."

"What more do you seek? She said she does not know your priestess."

"No. But I'm curious about her divination skills. Perhaps she will humor me and tell me my future."

With that, he retreated to the quarterdeck, leaving me staring out to sea before getting swept up in my daily tasks. I checked in on Siobhan once, finding her asleep when I brought her more broth and herbal tea.

Even after her kisses, her invitation to sleep together on the floor of the cabin came as a surprise, albeit a pleasant one. Now, I sit in the chair from the table, watching her snuggled in a mountain of old woolen blankets while she quietly sips the remainder of her tea. The later it gets the more nervous I find myself, which is ridiculous. I have lain with women in the past, but never one that caused my breath to hitch when she smiled at me, or that made my skin feel like I had caught fire with the barest touch. How am I ever going to get any sleep this close to her?

"Are you tired, Erik?" Siobhan's soft voice pulls my gaze to hers when she speaks.

"I am. Are you? Or would you like to take a walk on deck before turning in?" My body is weary after restless sleep on the floor of the Captain's cabin and, in truth, I would like to stretch out on the soft mattress after the nights on Lennox's rug.

"I'm tired, too. Should we go to bed?" Siobhan's cheeks flush slightly at her words, and my heart skips a beat. I told her I would not allow this to get physical while she is still recovering, and, although she has not coughed as much since she drank the tea laced with honey, she is still not fully recovered.

Soundlessly, she places the empty mug on the table and pulls her dress over her head. I am not sure if I remember to breathe until I see she has a thin shift under the garment that still covers her body. The material is thin enough to make out the curve of her breasts and a shadow of her nipples as she reaches back and unbinds her braid, running slim fingers through the red waves. As she stands before me, I cannot help but rake my eyes over her. She returns my gaze with a small smile before settling back down on her side of our pallet.

"Are you planning to sleep in your clothing, Erik? Or will you be sleeping in the chair?"

"I… uh… no." I stumble over my words as I remove my boots before standing. Then I pull my shirt over my head, noting her eyes traveling over my bare skin as I start to sit on the floor.

"Do you sleep in your breeches?" she asks.

When I look over at her I see that she is genuinely curious, not making advances. I am unable to fight my smile when I respond, "No, I usually sleep naked. But I did not think you would appreciate the insinuation if I were to strip all the way down."

"I would rather you be comfortable. This *is* your cabin after all." Her cheeks pink as she says the words, then adds, "I can turn around if you'd prefer," a broad smile spreading across her face.

"Siobhan, are you trying to get me naked in your bed?"

"I wouldn't be opposed to that turn of events." Her eyes have turned from guileless to heated as she speaks and I can see her nipples peak under the light shift she wears.

"I told you I would not take things further while you are still unwell. I am not sure me being nude would help me keep my word." *I am not that strong of a man*, I think.

"I promise to be on good behavior. See, I'll turn around." She turns her back to me with a light chuckle, then begins coughing as I unbutton my breeches. "Damn it," she curses under her breath, gripping a mug of water she kept ready off to the side. Dark whorls shadow the flesh of her back, suggestions of shapes decorating her skin, but I am more concerned about slipping under the blankets than studying her back at the moment.

Reclining on the mattress, I pull one of the woolen blankets over me, covering my legs and hips while she drinks, so that I am just as covered as I was in my breeches by the time her coughing subsides. The candlelight makes her fiery hair glimmer as she snuggles under her blanket, turning toward me. This close to her I can barely control the tremor in my muscles as I fight to keep from reaching out and pulling her close to me, trying to think of anything but the glimpse of her shape through the linen of her shift.

"Erik...?" she whispers as the candle burns low. I lay face up with my arm under my head, staring at the ceiling as the ship rocks beneath us, but turn my head to look into her eyes when she speaks.

"Yes?"

"Tell me about yourself," she murmurs. "We haven't had much time to speak to one another, what with me being sick and you being busy. Now that we are in such close quarters, I want to know you."

I blink a few times. It is rare to speak about myself, to speak much at all except to Lennox or the boatswain, Pike, these days. I carefully roll to face her, propping my head on a hand while she watches me. Her gaze is soft with sleepiness, but she still looks at me with interest, waiting for me to answer.

"What is it you wish to know?

"Who you are. Where do you come from? Why you're on this ship as a pirate instead of in the north as a trader or fisherman? Anything," she replies.

Taking a deep breath, I begin my story.

Tonight, I tell her about my family, my two older sisters and younger brother, my mother and father. How my father left one day on a regular voyage and the entire ship failed to return. I was fifteen then, my sisters were gone from the house, and my younger brother was wild and unruly. It fell to me to provide for my mother and brother until I left to sail on my own at seventeen. Siobhan listens intently, even though her eyes droop with sleep.

"We wrecked during one of the storms that can churn up suddenly. It forced us onto some rocks that our helmsman did not see in time. I was pulled out of the sea a day later by Captain Jackson. The captain of the *Selkie's Tears*," I explain. "It was on that ship I became a pirate and where I met Lennox after he mutinied on one of Blackwell's naval vessels a few years later."

"That sounds terrifying." Siobhan's eyes are wide at the description of the storm.

"It is something we have to get used to. Only the Goddess and the sea know our fate. We cannot fear what we do not control."

"Hmm," she replies. "Do you ever see your mother? Travel north?"

"Yes, she lives with her brother's family. She helps care for my cousin's children. My brother has wed by now, and may even have children of his own. We occasionally make it far enough north to see them, but it is not often. It has been over three years now." I miss my family, the crisp cold air, and the ice in the water, but this life I have found suits me, or it has so far.

Siobhan yawns, snuggling deeper into the blankets that surround her. "I'd like to see the lands to the far north. My mother said the skies dance there," she whispers, eyes fluttering with sleep. "Erik?"

"Yes?" Each time she says my name, my heart flutters like a moth trying to escape a lantern's flame, drawn to the light despite the potential to be burned.

"Sleep well. Thank you for sharing with me," she says softly. I am surprised when she rises from amongst her blankets and presses a chaste kiss on my cheek before curling up with her eyes closed. I do not know if she means sharing my stories or the cabin, but I try to calm my thundering heart to get some sleep.

CHAPTER 12
SIOBHAN

Lying next to Erik night after night as I fully recover from my illness is mildly torturous. His lilting accent soothes me as he tells me stories from his homeland before we fall asleep, even if his muscular frame is as taut as a cat ready to pounce the entire time we lay side by side talking. Each time I see his bare chest above the woolen blankets I long to reach out to explore the tattoos of runes and Northern designs marking the planes of his muscles under the dusting of dark hair. To press my lips against his skin to see how he tastes. To beg him to run his hands over my body like he did the day we kissed, like he does in my dreams. But Erik has held himself back from any further contact aside from innocent brushes, standing by his statement that he won't ask for more while I am still unwell — no matter how badly I may want him to break that promise.

The gentleness Erik has shown continues. He still measures out the herbs for my tea, even when I protest that I can do it myself. One night, after I'd begun to doze off, I caught him adjusting my blankets to be certain I was warm.

When I opened my eyes at the movement, he looked abashed and a blush painted his cheeks as he smiled at me, making my heart ache with pleasure. Sometimes, when the crash of the ocean worked more to keep me awake than to lull me to rest, I listened to him murmur in his native tongue in his sleep. These endearing moments, combined with our close proximity and increasingly frequent brushes of hands and bodies, make me desire nothing more than to pull him against me under our blankets.

After another week, my cough has vanished and I have more energy than I've had since living in the temple. I spend time on deck throughout the day, looking out at the vast ocean, soaking up the sea spray, and collecting new freckles under the bright sun, while the crew goes about their duties and Erik and Lennox spend time within the great cabin or talking to the men. As I study the crew, I notice some of the younger ones seem curious about me, not in a threatening way, but still more overtly than the hardened, sea-weathered men. Some tip their hats or bow in respect to me. One even shyly offered me an extra shift, though the Goddess knows where he found it, but they all give me a wide berth while they work. I make a note to speak with Erik tonight about their origins and beliefs when we have one of our nightly conversations. I look forward to our talks each evening, learning about him and drawing out his history when he's usually so reserved.

I spend most of my time sitting at the bow of the ship, near the figurehead. Even if she isn't real, isn't made of flesh and bone like my sisters were, she's still a comfort and a reminder of a life I cherished. Each day ends with us continuing to sail into the setting sun, the figurehead a dark outline bathed in warm pinks and oranges. I've tracked the moon phases since boarding the ship and the full moon is only a few days away, only the tiniest sliver of darkness still covers her face in the night sky. Relieved at my recovery, I plan to hold a small ceremony on the deck the night of the full moon, and I hope the men won't mind with their sailors' superstitions. None of them have dared to comment about a woman on board, and I've seen a few with tattoos that represent the Goddess, including Lennox himself, but I feel that asking permission is my safest option. I haven't been able to worship since I was forced into the camp, and a ripple of excitement tickles my skin at the thought of being free under the moon's glow. I hope I won't be denied.

As I wait for Erik to settle in for the night, I can't decide if I'm more interested in asking him about the full moon, or announcing that I'm no longer remotely ill. A flush burns in my cheeks as I turn to him, one that finally has nothing to do with a fever. His chest is already bare as he lies facing the ceiling, arm behind his head like he starts every night, trying to hide the restraint he exercises while resting so close to me. I sense that the flush on my cheeks and the heat that pools in my core is not a one-sided experience, but the tightness of tender emotions in my chest as I admire his profile might be. Pushing that thought aside, I focus on my shallow breaths before I speak.

"Erik?" My heart flutters as his breath catches on hearing his name.

"Siobhan?" he replies, turning his face toward me, the way we start our nights now a comfortable routine.

"I've been feeling much better the past couple of days," I whisper, hoping it doesn't sound as desperate with longing as I feel. The kisses we shared the day we began sharing this cabin, just under two weeks ago, only managed to strike a match in my veins and my needs have been smoldering ever since.

"I am glad to hear that," he says, his voice pitched lower than usual as his eyes flicker from mine to my lips and back.

I can't help but lick them as I ease my way closer to him under the warm blankets. He never takes his eyes off mine as he rolls to his side and reaches out to caress my hair with his calloused hand. The touch feels like lightning against my skin when he grazes his thumb across my cheekbone, then my lower lip, and my breath hitches. The next time he rubs his thumb across my lip I suck it into my mouth, tasting the ocean on his skin and earning a sharp gasp from the large man only an arm's length away.

We both move toward one another, closing the space between us swiftly as Erik tilts my head up with the same hand to capture my lips with his. My heart races wildly in my chest at the contact, my stomach flipping with the intensity of his kiss as I pull him closer, his warmth seeping through my thin shift as I press my breasts against him.

"Siobhan," Erik moans against my mouth between desperate kisses when I run my hand down his hard abdomen toward his thick erection. My nails graze the ridges of his muscles, tracing over raised scars and the edges of tattoos that punctuate his suntanned skin. He hisses through his teeth when my fingers dip below the edge of the blanket to stroke him.

I whimper unintelligibly as his large hands roam over me, skimming my thighs and rucking up my shift to grip my backside. He pulls me closer, pressing me against him while igniting all the sensitive parts of me. When he runs his tongue across my lips, opening them to him, wetness pools between my thighs, and I let out a soft moan. His beard chafes my smooth skin in the most glorious manner as he drags his mouth down my throat and pushes me onto my back so that he cages me with his forearms on either side of my head.

Carefully, so as to preserve one of the few garments I possess, he unlaces the top of my shift, pulling it off my shoulder with reverence as he reveals my breast in the candlelight. Staring up at him, all trace of the fearsome Northman seems to vanish. His eyes are soft as he takes me in, and his touch, while firm, is gentle when he cups my breast in his hand. I arch into his palm, circling my hips to tease his arousal. He groans in response, grinding against me.

Instead of lifting my shift to slide against me, he rolls to rest at my side, dragging his hand from my breast down my side and under my shift. His fingers deftly run up my thigh and through my wetness causing me to whimper with need.

"Erik," I breathe, lifting my hips in invitation again.

"I want to take my time, Siobhan. There's no rush," he murmurs against my neck. "Let me savor you." He slides his fingers against me once more before slipping one inside. As he curls his finger within me, he deepens our kisses, then slides his mouth down my neck, trailing a line that sends pleasant shivers over my skin with his teeth and tongue. "You're so wet. Have you been wanting this for as long as I have?" he asks against the shell of my ear.

"Yes," I reply. "Erik, I want all of you."

"You'll get what you want, Siobhan," he says nuzzling my neck. "I'll make sure you get everything you want."

He increases his pace, pressing against the apex of my thighs with his palm while still sliding his finger inside of me until I shudder and cry out, my muscles rippling while pleasure radiates from his touch. As I lay there shattered, Erik slides his hand from me, planting gentle kisses on my mouth and cheeks. Rolling toward him, I pull him closer, returning his kisses and running my fingers over the velvety stubble that grows on the sides of his scalp, tracing the dark lines of his tattoos underneath. Resting my head on his broad chest I listen to his heart race while I trail my touch over the dusting of hair that covers his chest and stomach. To my surprise and dismay, as I reach below the blanket, he pulls away from me as if he plans to roll over to sleep.

"Erik?" My voice is rough in the dim cabin.

"Yes?"

"What about you?" I sit up, propped on my elbows in confusion.

"I can wait. I do not wish to tire you out too much in one night when you have only just recovered." He leans across me with a sly smile, slowly sucking my nipple into his mouth while looking up into my eyes, before pulling my shift back over my breast. "We have plenty of time for me to have my pleasure, Siobhan. Tonight, it was enough to finally touch you." My stomach clenches as he drags his thumb over my hardened nipple once more, and then kisses me deeply.

"Goodnight, Siobhan."

Catching my breath, I whisper back, "Goodnight," and tuck myself against him, wiggling my backside against his groin and earning a huff of amusement from him in return. Instead of proceeding as I hoped he would, Erik simply wraps one arm around me, holding me tight as he curls his body to fit mine. Within minutes, I let sleep drag me under with a smile still firmly upon my lips.

CHAPTER 13
ERIK

Siobhan's quiet breathing is less labored than it has been on previous nights as she lays curled asleep at my side. Her cough is all but completely gone and she sleeps more soundly than she has since we began sharing these quarters. A smile twitches the corner of my mouth at the thought that perhaps I had something to do with easing her to sleep tonight. The creak of the ship and the familiar sounds of the open sea all settle around me as I stare into the darkness.

I know I should sleep. Lennox has cut none of my duties on this voyage and, between the tasks on deck and lying awake next to Siobhan, I am exhausted. She has rolled away from me in sleep, resting on her stomach with her lips parted. I long to wrap my arms around her and bury my face in her hair to smell the sweet herbal scent. I want to hold her against me to comfort myself as much as to comfort her. But I will not risk waking her, even if she has made it more than clear she desires my attention. I do not wish for her to think I am asking for more in the middle of the night. Not when what I find I truly want is likely beyond reach for the two of us.

I roll to my side, facing her as she sleeps and carefully reach my fingers out to touch a strand of her copper hair. The barest touch has her eyes flickering open, but before I can draw back, worried she will be afraid, she smiles dreamily and scoots closer to me once more, cuddling against my chest and murmuring something under her breath before she is asleep again, offering me the closeness I had hoped for. I barely breathe as she settles against me, and then, draping my arm over her I drift off to a contented sleep, too.

SUNLIGHT STREAMS THROUGH THE SMALL PORTHOLE IN OUR cabin when I wake. The sounds of footsteps on the decks rattle above us as the crew moves about, but Siobhan still lies curled at my side, eyes closed against the morning. Her ginger lashes lay across her freckle-dusted cheeks and her pink lips are parted slightly as she breathes. Watching her sleep causes something in my chest to ache. Holding my breath, I reach out and caress her bare shoulder, wanting nothing more than to trace between each freckle that dots her skin.

I never expected to find a woman in the alley when we tracked the soldiers in Athene, and when we did, I never expected her to be anything different than the other women Lennox has ferried across the sea. But now, I catch myself wanting to be with her instead of tending to my duties, wanting to hear her brogue tell me about her childhood, her training, her favorite things. Wanting to touch her and hold her and protect her. The ache deepens when I remind myself that my life is on the sea and hers is on land. I cannot bear to think of what we will do when those decisions are made.

I do not have any more time to consider such things as the sun rises. I slip from the blankets and dress quickly, pulling my shirt over my head as Siobhan begins to stir.

"Good morning, Erik," she mumbles, rubbing sleep from her eyes and sitting up. Her shift hangs from one creamy shoulder and the memory of it pulled farther down last night makes me ache.

"Good morning," I reply, kneeling at her side. I know growing closer to her will only make it harder to part on Delosia, but it has been so long since I have had someone to freely share affection with and I find I miss it. Reaching out I cup her cheek and she grins in response, encouraging me to pull her closer and take her mouth with mine. A little noise in the back of her throat has me deepening our embrace as I pull her against me. We break apart when a tap comes at the door, breathing hard at the interruption.

"Yes?" I call out, clearing my voice as I run my thumb over her cheek.

"Quartermaster, we need you on deck. Give your lady a break!" Lennox's deep voice teases, but an undercurrent of command is clear in his tone.

"Aye, Captain," I return, moving to stand from Siobhan's side. "I will be back when I can," I say to her before turning to open the door and walk into the hold beyond.

At the top of the stairs, Lennox's golden head catches my eye where he waits for me on deck with Pike. Both men's eyes glisten with amusement as I approach, but Pike excuses himself with a dip of the head when I reach them.

"How's our priestess doing, Quartermaster? Hopefully, you aren't too worn out from your evening activities," he drawls as I reach his side.

"What did you need, Captain?"

"Erik? Are you all right?" Lennox rakes his eyes over my face, all signs of teasing gone. He may project cocky confidence, but he is far more in tune with his crew than they even know, especially those of us who are closest to him.

"I am fine, Captain. Why?"

"You look like you'd like to take a swing at me is why. I meant no disrespect to Siobhan, you know that."

"I do."

Changing the subject, Lennox hands me his spyglass and nods toward the horizon. "Should we take her?" Raising the glass to my eye, I spot the vessel in question – a merchant ship. "Or do you think the risk is too great with your priestess on board?"

I grit my teeth at his question. Normally, there wouldn't be a concern, we would immediately raise the black and take the ship. I do not want to risk Siobhan, but I know the crew will be eager for a prize, and a merchant ship is less likely to cause damage than one of the naval vessels Lennox usually hunts.

"Let's take it. But let me explain to her what to do. I will be back." Lennox nods once in acceptance and I turn to return to my cabin.

When I enter the room, Siobhan has dressed and sits at the table braiding her hair while a small bowl of porridge rests in front of her. She beams at me so brightly when I open the door that my heart stutters at her happiness. I find myself returning her smile, but it fades quickly as I close the door and approach to explain to her about the merchant ship.

"And you're certain I won't be taken?" her voice falters as she asks me again, even if she tries to hide the tremble of her hands.

"I promise you; no one will take you. You will remain in this cabin. Merchant ships usually surrender without a struggle. We will load the goods and be on our way," I reassure her again. The fear in her eyes makes me want to return to the deck to tell Lennox it is not worth the prize, but I cannot do that to the entire crew just to ease my own heart. I am confident she will be safe, as long as she stays below and out of sight.

"I trust you. I'll stay below." Siobhan accepts the plan, but her eyes still hold the glint of panic I saw in the alley and I hate myself for having to leave her below deck alone. I gather my axes, tucking them into their holders – one at my hip and one at my lower back, then fasten my vambraces. Before leaving I pull Siobhan close, holding her tight against me for a moment before pressing a kiss against her soft mouth.

When I return above deck Lennox is giving commands, his leather greatcoat swirling in the breeze as the black flag rises into the air. Although I expect this to be a simple merchant raid, his eyes already have the vicious gleam I am used to seeing when he expects more violence to come. I trust him, but I hope no soldiers protect the merchant vessel or more blood will spill than is truly necessary.

As the merchant ship comes into view, the men on board lower their sails, slowing their progress in response to our approach. The sight of Lennox's wolf skull flag has achieved its goal, his reputation growing more fearsome with each voyage. Perhaps this will go smoothly, after all.

CHAPTER 14
SIOBHAN

I alternate sitting at the little table in our cabin with pacing the floor and wringing my hands. I've already folded our extra blankets and stacked them on one of the bunks, brushed and re-braided my hair, and pulled on my hand-me-down boots just in case I need to flee. Anything to occupy my hands and mind while sailors stomp the deck overhead and faint shouts drift on the breeze. But nothing soothes my nerves, least of all the fact that my porthole looks out to the open ocean, not the merchant ship we've sidled up to.

Erik promised I would be safe, but will *he*?

The pleasure from the night before, the hope and warmth that filled me when he held me last night and kissed me this morning has faded into a pit of fear in my chest waiting for him to return. Is this how it feels waiting for your man to return to you when your heart belongs to a sailor?

I don't know what his feelings are for me — whether he merely finds me attractive and warm for the voyage, or if he has the same growing emotions that I do — but I will regret it deeply if he should be harmed without us having discussed them. Even though it's only been a short time, I know in my soul that he was meant to find me. That we were meant to find one another.

The tromp of boots becomes more numerous overhead, and I hold my breath while shouts grow louder. Closer. Panic raises a sour taste in my mouth at the thought of our ship being boarded, or of strangers taking me from the safety of my cabin. Footsteps echo in the hold outside my door, and I clutch a small knife I pulled from Erik's trunk in my trembling hand, waiting for the door to open. When it does, relief floods me and I relax. The doorway is filled with the tall frame of my Northman. Beads of sweat cover him, but he doesn't appear worse for the wear as he meets my eyes.

"Erik!" I exclaim, rushing toward him and throwing my arms around his waist.

"It is done, Siobhan. You can come above now if you wish," he says, brushing his hand down the back of my head in comfort as he holds me.

Nodding, I follow Erik up the stairs to find a flurry of activity. Our crew shouts in excitement as they look over their prize, explaining the raised voices I heard below. The merchant ship sits forlornly in the water off our side, drifting farther away with each wave, its crew and captain bound, but alive, on the deck.

"You didn't kill them?" I ask, surprised at the lack of bloodshed. All the rumors I'd heard of pirates were filled with debauchery and cruelty, but standing amongst them I realize they're just men, like any others. Just like the northern raiders given a terrifying reputation regardless of their guilt.

"No." Erik scans the crew as they group crates according to the orders shouted by Lennox and an older dark-skinned man who stands beside him. "We do not kill the merchants unless they try to kill us first. Lennox only brings death to Blackwell's ships, or those he deems deserve it. This captain was reasonable and only transported spices and alcohol."

"Was anyone hurt?"

"One of our crew took a hard blow early on, another a blade to the arm. Nothing serious."

"May I see them? To be certain?"

Erik looks down at me, drawing his attention fully from the others with a warm smile. "Of course."

He leads me past sailors carrying crates and sacks of foodstuffs down into the hold to the bow of the ship where two crewmen wait away from the bustle of the others. One holds a bloody rag against his wounded shoulder and the other sits with his back against the side of a crate with one eye swelling closed from the blow Erik described.

"Siobhan will tend to your injuries," Erik tells them, causing both to perk up a bit. "Do you need anything?" he asks me.

"A bottle of strong alcohol," I reply, crouching down to inspect the sailor with the black eye first. "And a small, sharp blade," I add, determining that I must lance the injury or else he'll lose sight in the eye for days waiting for the swelling to go down. "Oh!" I exclaim as I turn to the other sailor, pulling the rag gently from their arm to find a much deeper injury to the shoulder than I expected.

"And a needle and thread. Better bring two bottles of alcohol."

Erik responds with a dip of his chin before he retreats below deck to gather the supplies.

"Nice to finally meet you, mistress," the sailor with the shoulder injury says, smiling genuinely as though the pain of the injury is nothing more than a flesh wound. The high-pitched voice makes me squint to look closer under the knit cap covering messy blond hair. At the sight of my eyes widening, the sailor laughs, a tinkling sound so at odds with the rough clothing of a pirate. "Aye, I would have thought you'd know by now since you've taken up with Varangr. I'm a woman."

"Oh!" I'm embarrassed that it's taken me this long to realize what should have been obvious. It *would* have, had I not been so ill and hidden away. Looking across the decks I smile, my eyes landing on the young "men" to realize that several are not men at all. "Well, this *is* a surprise!"

"You're telling me." The man with the black eye says with a chuckle. "Took me a week to figure out why this one wouldn't just strip down to change clothes. Imagine my surprise when I turned around one day to find out she's got tits!"

"You watch your mouth in front of the priestess, you shit," the woman scolds, tossing her bloodied rag at his bad side so he can't see it well enough to catch it. They both laugh heartily and I can't help but join in.

"What's happening here?" Lennox's voice is rough behind me, drawing my eye to both him and Erik standing with curious looks on their faces.

"Just finding out that some of your crew is of the female

persuasion, Captain," I reply, standing to take the bottles and supplies from Erik's hands. "Thank you, Erik. I can handle it from here."

"I will assist Pike with the rest," Erik tells Lennox, then joins the older man I saw with Lennox earlier near the center mast.

"Thank you, Siobhan. Please let me know if you require anything else," Lennox says, his voice gentle. "And thank you both. You'll each receive an extra drink tonight should you want it. For your troubles."

Both sailors incline their heads, smiling at their captain before he too joins the other men.

"Forgive me, I haven't asked your names. I'm Siobhan," I introduce myself to my two patients, giving each of them a heavy pour of drink to dull the pain of what I need to do.

"I'm Fiona and this is Aiden," the woman replies. "You hang in there, man," she adds, squeezing Aidan's hand before I slice into the dark purple swell of his skin, releasing thick blood to ease the swelling. Placing a folded cloth over it, I direct him to hold it with his free hand as he stifles a groan and grips tight to Fiona. "Will you be joining the crew then, Mistress Siobhan?" she asks while I thread a needle for her arm, looking anywhere but at the needle or her injury.

"Me? I'm no sailor. I'm surprised I've managed to keep from being seasick, to tell the truth," I answer, but my heart stutters a bit at the thought of staying. Sharing a bed each night with Erik's warm body by my side might be enough of a reason to consider it. Could I do it?

"Oh, I see. I just thought… Are you not with the quartermaster, then? I thought that was the way of it. The other priestesses usually stay alone, and he's a right fine man." Fiona hisses through her teeth as I pour some of the whiskey over her wound, and then begin to stitch it closed.

"I… well… I suppose we'll see, won't we."

When Fiona's wound is stitched and wrapped with clean linen and Aiden's eye has opened, they both resume their duties as best as they can, leaving me to clean up the mess from their healing. Pride and comfort both find me as I rinse their blood from my hands and tidy the bloody rags from the deck. It feels familiar to be healing again, to be able to help allies instead of enemies, to honor my strengths and skills without fear always in my gut. All that's missing is a stock of herbs and a group of priestesses by my side, and I'd almost think I was back at the temple.

My mind wanders to Fiona's question about my future as I gather my things. Would I be happy living on a ship? Does Erik even want that?

I've always loved the sea, getting lost in the sight and sounds of the waves hitting the shore of Airmedan, but always with my feet firmly on land. This is the first time I've been so far from the earth, and now, without Erik to distract me, I realize how far we are from land in any direction. I shake off the tension, standing and staring into the waves. It's silly of me to be lost in these worries anyway, I have no idea what is to become of Erik, or where exactly we are destined. Better to focus on the moment than think too far ahead. Reminding myself that all will work out as it should, I carry my supplies below deck while the sailors settle back to their usual routines.

"THE MOON IS FULL SOON," I MENTION AS I SPOON SALTED meat and boiled grain into my mouth that evening. This is the first night we've dined in the main mess area of the ship. Since I tended to the wounded today, Erik asked if I would like to join them all instead of remaining in our room. While I enjoy our private time together, I agreed, if only to see the rest of the "men" relaxed and celebrating.

"It is." Erik sits next to me at the end of a table filled with Lennox, Pike – the older man Erik helped on deck earlier, the ship's boatswain – and a few other crewmen. Erik smiles indulgently at my statement, as though he already knows where this conversation is heading. He's eating a similar ration and drinking a cup of rum. I haven't partaken in the stronger alcohol, but Erik obtained some watered-down wine for me from Captain Lennox as a reward for my work on the crew earlier, and I already feel a pleasant warmth spreading from the half a glass I have consumed.

"Do you think it would be all right if I were to pray on deck that night?"

"Of course. Lennox holds the Old Ways, he wouldn't deny you that," Erik advises over the din of the crowded space.

"I guess I should have assumed as much, but I wasn't sure if he would mind." I direct my gaze toward the captain who is deep in conversation with Pike. I would ask him, but I don't want to interrupt, and now that my bowl is done and the wine has made my limbs loose, I want to escape back to the comfort of our cabin.

"No one will bother you, Siobhan. You are welcome to do as you like aboard. This is your home until we reach

Delosia." Erik smiles at me as he finishes his rum, blue eyes crinkling at the corners when I smile back.

Until we reach Delosia.

"Can we go back to our room, now?" I ask, my mood sobering at the mention of our destination. "I'm tired."

Erik stands, taking my hand to help me to my feet, and then we slip through the tables. The crew continues to talk, but many nod and smile at me as we pass, making my heart warm with growing affection for them.

After undressing and settling in, we spend the rest of the evening quietly tucked into our blankets until the candle burns low and exhaustion from the unusually busy day overtakes us.

THE DAY OF THE FULL MOON FINDS ME RESTLESS. I'M BOTH anxious and excited to be able to freely pray under the moon and stars again after being trapped in the army camp where it was never safe for me to be out in the darkness alone. Erik mentioned that Lennox holds the Old Ways, but didn't mention himself. I know the people of the Northern Isles believe in the Goddess, but I don't pry. A part of me wants to be sure I remember my ceremony, that I remember the way it feels to be surrounded by the moonlight, before asking him to join me.

That evening though, I wonder, Will I have another full moon with him? Or is this my only chance? Now that the idea of us parting has sunk in, I can't seem to escape it, and the thought brings a pain to my chest as I gather a candle, a goblet of wine, and some of the sweet-smelling herbs I have left from the packet I purchased in Athene. Erik and I ate a quiet meal in our cabin and he smiles at me now as I head toward the door with my items, but doesn't make a move to come with me.

"Enjoy your moon, Siobhan," he murmurs as I reach the door.

"Thank you, Erik," I reply, smiling and drifting into the hold.

Climbing the stairs, I find the decks almost empty. Most of the crew is down in the dining area at this hour. The sight of the full moon over the ocean makes my breath catch in my chest. The white glow reflects off the dark water as it ripples around us and the stars blaze in the black sky. Tears seep from my eyes as I take in the sight, standing still on the main deck holding my supplies with the briny breeze blowing my hair gently around me. I look around, trying to determine the most appropriate place when I realize the perfect spot.

The bow. Next to the priestess figurehead.

I may not have any sister priestesses with me to perform the ceremony, but she can be my quiet companion as I remind myself what it feels like to be free again. I wasn't trained as a high priestess. I usually joined in the ceremonies, adding my voice and energy to the group while our High Priestess led, but I never led them myself. This will be the first time I've done it alone.

My mind wanders to nights in the temple as I stride toward the bow, memories of dancing with my friends in the sacred grove under the night skies, drinking wine and offering honeyed fruit and cakes to the Goddess, making love under the stars when suitors might come to beg favors from the Goddess and her priestesses. The memory of being lost in a lover's arms grips me as I think of Erik, waiting in our quiet cabin below, distracting me so much that I almost shriek when a dark figure rises from the deck next to the figurehead.

"Priestess." Captain Lennox's voice drifts from the shadow. "I didn't mean to startle you." When he stands to his full height his burnished hair shines in the moonlight, eyes dark in the shadows.

"Captain! I wasn't expecting you here, am I interrupting? I can go somewhere else." I know Erik told me the captain wouldn't mind, but I never asked outright, and now I worry I should have.

"Nonsense, Siobhan. I hoped I would find you here after Erik confirmed you would be allowed to celebrate the full moon tonight."

For a brief moment, I fear his implication. Surely, he doesn't intend to lay with me in offering as some men did at the temple. He has to know Erik would never allow that. Nor would I.

"Wipe that scared look off your face, please. I have no intention of seducing you in the moonlight, Siobhan," Lennox scoffs, smiling at me as my eyes widen. "I know better than to challenge Erik for you. Plus, you aren't the priestess I've been looking for."

"Oh, I… of course not…" I don't know how to respond, opening and closing my mouth as I try to think of something to say. Thankfully, Lennox continues before I have to say anything.

"I merely hoped you would allow me to sit with you

while you honor the Goddess. It's been a very long time since I've witnessed it."

"Of course, Captain. Whatever you wish."

With that, he melts back down to the deck, leaning his back against the hull and tilting his head against the rail to stare up at the sky. Like this, with the cocky grin wiped away he looks sad. Lonely. Almost as though he is as lost as I've felt these past years.

I light my candle, then pour a small amount of wine in offering on the deck, drinking some before adding the herbs and saying a prayer over it. Chanting in the ancient language of the Goodess, I dump the contents of the goblet into the sea. As I continue to pray, I find that the words come back to me quickly, ending the chant and beginning a song. I'm surprised when I hear the lyrics whispered in a singsong from Lennox as he joins me.

When I look over at him, I almost stop singing. Tears run from his closed eyes and over his hollow cheeks while his full lips murmur the words in time with me. It's clear this man has lost more than a mystery woman over these past years, but I maintain my song, harmonizing with him until the end.

"Captain?" I ask hesitantly while he sits in silence.

"You can call me William. You don't have to call me Captain, Siobhan. At least not when we speak plainly," he replies, wiping the tears roughly from his face as he sits straighter to look at me. "And thank you. It's been a while since I heard the old language sung in a woman's voice. Not since I last saw my mother." His voice catches at the word and my heart aches for him and his obvious sorrow.

"Was she a believer?"

"She was a priestess. I found her body burned in front of our home. I couldn't protect her from them, and couldn't protect myself from them either. But I think you'll agree that isn't the case anymore." His eyes harden, all sadness erased by wrath, as he shares his story. I reach out tentatively to pat one of his hands where it rests on his knee and he gives a lopsided smile. "Thank you, Siobhan."

"Perhaps a song my mother used to sing to me would make your heart hurt a bit less? Even if just for tonight?" I don't know what possessed me to offer this song, what makes me ask if I can sing it to him, but even if this man has proven himself to be a brutal killer, I don't believe that's his true nature. It's who he's been made into over these years, who any of us could become.

He gives a small nod and I begin to sing my mother's lullaby.

CHAPTER 15
ERIK

After Siobhan departed, I waited for ten minutes to give her time to settle on deck. I was not sure how long she would need to perform her ceremony and I did not want to be a distraction, but I longed to see the moon myself and to see the joy on her face at being under the bright glow at sea.

Climbing the stairs to the deck, I scanned the space until I saw her outlined in the moonlight near the bow. But she is not alone. Standing at the rail talking to her is Lennox. I knew he would likely come out to see the moon, just like I did, and to maybe pour an offering over the railing, but I cannot fathom why he would be with Siobhan. I am even more confused when I see him sit back down against the side of the ship while she fusses with her supplies.

After she gives her offering, her voice floats on the gentle breeze as she begins to chant and Lennox leans his head back, eyes closed, listening. I know he still suffers from finding his mother's body and mourns her and the life he dreamed of having before everything changed. I was there when he went into a fit of rage afterward and almost beat a priest to death when we came upon him in the nearby village. But, despite knowing my friend needs this catharsis, I am jealous that he sits so close to her, hearing her words and feeling the comfort that I long for.

I am a fool.

If I had just told her earlier that I wanted to come with her she would have allowed it. Instead, I stayed silent, and now I am huddled like a spymaster trying to gather information instead of sitting next to my friend, listening to my… *what*? *Lover*?

As I wrestle with my thoughts, Siobhan's voice changes to a song and I can just make out Lennox's voice joining hers. Once the song ends, I start to stand to join them, but pause when Siobhan reaches out to pat Lennox's hand. She says a few quiet words to him before she starts another song and my heart nearly stops.

This is not a song of the Goddess.

This is not even a song of Selennia.

This is a song of the Northern Isles. A song of my people, my home, my family.

The lullaby I hummed to her while she was sick with fever.

A Northman's lullaby.

But, how? I never sang the words aloud; I am sure of it. How does she know them?

The song ends quickly and I watch as Lennox stands to leave. He says a few words quietly to Siobhan, then turns and walks away without a backward glance. I rise to my feet as Lennox approaches, but he does not look surprised.

"Making sure I wasn't inappropriate with your woman,

Erik?" he chides, but there is no heart in his words. I can see the hollow look in his eyes and know the sideways smile he gives is only for show. My friend hides his hurts well most of the time, but not tonight. "Go to her, you fool. Or I just might change my mind and decide she *is* the right priestess for me after all." He chucks me on the shoulder in jest, then continues his walk to his cabin.

Siobhan kneels on the deck, staring at the bright moon when I approach. Her back is to me, but she turns her face just enough that she can see me approach and a smile lifts the edge of her lips when I near.

"Have you come to join me?"

"How did you know that song?" I ask without preamble. I have to know.

"Which song?"

"You know which song, Siobhan."

"You hummed it to me when I was sick." She turns to face me now, still looking up at me from the damp planks of the deck. The moon shines down on her, casting her cheekbones and the copper of her hair in a silver glow. I imagine it is how her own *glow* would have looked using her power in the temple.

"I never sang the words. How do you know them?"

"My mother. She sang it to me as a child. She and my grandfather and my uncles all came from the north." Her voice is soft, but steady as she tells me her family's story. "My grandfather moved them to Selennia after my grandmother passed away in a hard childbirth. My mother married a Selennian man in a village near the Northern Point and they had me, but she was always so homesick. She said that song was a song of home."

Siobhan's eyes rake over my face, trying to read my expression as she speaks. I sink to my knees on the deck in front of her, grasping her hands in mine as she breathlessly continues, "It's why I wasn't afraid of you in the alley. Why I trusted *you* instead of Lennox. You look like my family. And when I heard you humming that song when I was sick. Well…" She pauses, her hands tremble slightly, but her eyes look straight into mine as she says, "You feel like home, Erik. Like you were meant for me."

My heart pounds in my chest, even more so than when she merely wanted me to touch her. Now her words make my heart ache with want for her. Because I feel the same way. This woman fills an emptiness I never realized I had until now. I have no idea how I will be able to keep her after this, but I know I have to try. Cupping her face in my hand, I tilt it so I can kiss her, gently at first, then with urgency as she grips the linen of my shirt in her slender fingers. I scoop her into my arms as I stand, cradling her to my chest as I follow the silver light of the moon leading toward the stairs, as though the moon herself is guiding my steps, then descend into the hold to our shared quarters.

I kick the door closed behind me when we enter the small cabin, still holding Siobhan tight to me as she gasps and a giggle escapes her full lips. She slips from my arms and pulls my face down to hers, while I run my hands through her fiery hair and down her back, her skin pebbling as she shivers from my touch. Her hands trail down my chest, then my stomach until they reach my waistband. She tugs my shirt from my pants and pushes it upwards, murmuring, "Off." A chuckle escapes me as I pull it over my head and toss it into the corner. As it hits the floor, she begins unbuttoning my pants, her bright blue eyes looking up at me with a glint of mischief shining behind them.

"Tonight, I want you to give me everything I want, Erik. All of you." She smiles, her teeth glistening on the edge of her lower lip as she bites it and runs her hand under my pants to grip me. I suck in a breath at her warm touch, groaning as she runs her hand along my cock.

"What about what I want?" I murmur, tilting my head back as she continues to stroke me.

"You can have whatever you want from me." Her voice is sultry, and in my surprise at her offer, I snap my head down to look at her, finding desire that matches my own in her eyes. I reach down and pull her hand from my pants, stepping back to sit on the hard wooden edge of the empty bunk on the left side of the room.

"Take off your dress," I tell her as she stands in the center of the cabin. Her breath is shaky as she unclasps the bodice and slips her dress from her body, kicking it to the side of our pallet, eyes never leaving mine. Her sheer shift barely hides her form. "Now your shift."

A smile quirks her pink lips and I know she is putting on a show as she slowly unties the neck of her shift, sliding the shoulder off one side, then the other so it languidly slips from her breasts, her waist, her hips, and to the floor. Her creamy skin is luminous in the candlelight, and I want nothing more than to pull her to me and fuck her immediately, but I hold myself back as I take in her soft curves.

"Your turn, Erik. Take off your pants," she boldly commands, taking a step toward me. I kick out of my boots and stand, pushing my pants off, so we are both naked and trembling with restraint. Her eyes roam over me as if I haven't laid naked next to her night after night trying to keep my hands to myself.

"Come here." I reach out to pull her closer, gripping her small hand in my rough palm as I pull her against me. Her soft breasts press against my firm torso as our mouths crash together.

Finally, the restraint we have both clung to dissolves in a clash of teeth and tongues as we explore one another. Soft noises in the back of her throat have me groaning in response. I reach down, caressing her backside with my hands before sliding them to grip her under her thighs to lift her up. Siobhan digs her fingers into my shoulders as she wraps her legs around my waist, nuzzling against my throat and peppering it with open-mouthed kisses. At this angle, my cock teases her entrance, and the slick heat between her legs makes me want to take her against the wall without another thought, her panting breaths against my ear urging me to do just that. But, she's so small and I want to be sure she's comfortable, so I lower her to her feet, then kneel, tugging her down to the soft mattresses beneath me.

CHAPTER 16
SIOBHAN

Erik pulls me down to the pallet next to him, so that we both kneel. I would have happily allowed him to have his way with me against the wall moments ago, but I knew he would hold himself back, just like he has the entire time we've lain together night after night. His need is clear and his eyes are ablaze as they rake over me.

I'm tired of waiting.

Gripping his neck I pull his mouth to mine, our lips slanting against one another as he wraps his arms around me, pressing me against his body. When we part, I look into his eyes, our breath mingling as we pant. "Erik, I need you."

My words seem to ignite something behind his eyes and he claims my mouth with a deep kiss as he pulls me toward him, laying on his back and holding me so that I straddle him, pressing against his hard length. I roll my hips against him, sliding him against the wetness between my thighs as I sit up. Erik's rough hands grip my hips as he watches me, then trail over my stomach and up to my breasts, exploring my skin with their calloused warmth. I lean down once more, kissing him deeply before sitting back up and rising to slide him into me, his eyes focused on my face.

Erik groans with a ragged exhale as his head tips back and he grips my hips. It takes a few moments for me to be seated fully, his size stretching and filling me with a pleasant sting at first, and drawing a whimper from me. It's been an age since I've been with a man and I realize how much I've missed the passion between lovers as we slide together. I dip my chin, a soft moan escaping my lips as I begin to rock my hips.

"*Fuck*, Siobhan," Erik moans, his long fingers squeezing my backside as he guides my motion. Then he sits up, pulling my face to his and kissing me as I wrap my legs around his hips and continue to ride him. Pleasure coils in my belly as we move together, Erik trailing hot kisses down my throat, sucking at the place it meets my shoulder. As my climax nears, I can't stop my moans as the rhythm increases, dragging my fingernails over his broad shoulders as I clutch him closer.

"*Erik*, please don't stop," I cry as I shatter around him, stifling my moans against his neck. He holds me against him for a moment as I catch my breath, then flips me onto my back. He gently presses his lips against mine, then drags them to my neck, then lower, his beard tickling down to my breasts where he pauses to pull one of the peaked nipples into his mouth. As he looks up at me, I buck my hips in question, earning a grin from him as he continues to trail kisses down to my belly and then my inner thigh.

Suddenly, he sits back on his heels and flips me so I'm face down on the mattress, pressing his mouth against my backside, my lower back, and then breathes against the column of my neck as I bare it to him to look over my shoulder. He gazes at my back, trailing his fingers over the tattoos that are finally on display to him, those which my uncle and mother placed lovingly on my skin with blessings before I left to live in the temple. The same types of designs that he wears on his own flesh.

With his arousal pressed against my backside, I smile and arch my back to tease him with my behind, refocusing his attention so that he moans into my hair as he grinds against me. He plants open-mouthed kisses on my back, then runs his tongue along my neck, nibbling at the place it meets my shoulder. I tremble with need and my core aches for him. Pulling my hips up he teases my entrance before siding back inside of me as I grip the sheets, twisting them in my fingers, and gasp into the mattress. This time there is no sting from him filling me as he thrusts deep, one hand on my lower back and the other on my hip.

Erik increases his rhythm and reaches around to press against the apex of my thighs, drawing moans from me at the pleasant friction as he circles with his rough fingers until I near my release once more, my cries muffled in the mattress. As I find my pleasure again, Erik increases his tempo, his ragged breathing mingling with mine. But when I expect him to finish, he pulls away from me, and the warmth of his release spills on my lower back.

Erik's rapid breathing echoes through the cabin as I lay flat on my belly, trying to catch my breath and clinging to the warmth swirling in my breast from my happiness. Erik kisses my shoulder, then wipes my back with a soft cloth before he lays next to me, tossing it aside before running his hand through my loose waves.

When I curl on my side to face him, Erik's smile is soft as he studies me. "I was not sure if you had the herbs for the preventative tea. I did not want to assume," he whispers in explanation.

"That's very thoughtful of you." I snuggle against his side, tucked under his arm with my cheek pressed against his chest so I can feel his heart pounding beneath the muscle. His fingers wrap in my loose hair, aimlessly stroking the strands, and soothing me more than I've been in years.

"I am glad I found you, Siobhan."

"I am too, Erik."

We spend that night and those that follow, wrapped around one another. Long limbs and sated sighs bring us closer than I've ever been with another person, but each dawn when Erik dresses and kisses me before returning to his duties brings a different thought. One that becomes louder with each day we draw closer to the island of Delosia.

What happens next?

CHAPTER 17
ERIK

Another week or so is all we have before our feet will be on the sands of Delosia instead of the planks of the ship. I cut my eyes to Siobhan, staring at the darkening horizon by my side. I have no idea how I am supposed to introduce her to the island and then leave her there. Mistress Marie leads the people now, and I know she is a fierce protector of the inhabitants, but my regret and indecision nag at my thoughts, nonetheless.

"Erik!" Lennox calls over the crack of the sails to snap me back to the present. "Get Siobhan below, now!" A squall line looms black on the horizon, something we hoped we would not see this time of year, but the risk is always present.

"What on earth is *that*?" Siobhan grips my sleeve, knuckles white as she points to a twisting funnel dropping from the edge of the black clouds.

"Nothing good. Come on," I answer, grabbing her hand and pulling her along to the stairs. Now, the worry over saying goodbye is eclipsed by a rising panic in my chest, we will not have to worry about Delosia if we do not make it through this storm first.

"Erik?" The uncertainty in Siobhan's voice causes my heart to clench when we stumble into our cabin. Her breath is shaky and her eyes are glassy and wide like a cornered hare when I turn to pull her close.

"It will be all right, my love," I answer, cupping her cheek. "You must stay here for now, you will be safe. I will be back as soon as possible."

She nods her head in response, even as she trembles, then squeezes me and lets me go.

"I understand. Be safe, Erik."

Before leaving her, I stroke my hand over her hair, cradling her cheeks before I tilt her chin up and kiss her, intending for it to be a quick touch, but she wraps her arms around my neck, returning my kiss with a ferocity I did not realize she possessed.

"Come back to me," she whispers against my lips.

"Always."

Leaving her is difficult, seeing her blue eyes full of fear is almost physically painful, but I close the cabin door and climb the stairs to the deck to join Lennox as the storm begins to bear down on us in earnest. I am forced to grip tight to the rain-slicked railing as I climb, steadying myself as the ship rocks violently and the rain stings my cheeks.

The funnel rises and lowers from the black clouds, tearing at the canvas and tossing the ship over the rough waters as rains pummel us. At least this far from land we do not risk hitting any landmasses or other ships, and our hull is laden to keep us steady, but many of the crewmembers lash themselves to the ship with rope to remain on board just in case.

Shouting over the wind, I instruct the helmsman to turn us, encouraging him to sail at an angle to the storm as much as possible while Pike's deep timbre booms at the men trying to take down the sails to save them from more serious damage. Lennox's soaked form is barely visible through the rain alongside his men, fighting the sea and storm. Each of us struggles against the rain and wind to stay standing and to keep our crew from toppling over the railing.

In the chaos, one of the ropes swings loose, the heavy end slamming into one of the crewmen. He careens on deck, sliding helplessly as the ship lists to the side. Without hesitation, I dash across the deck, losing my footing and sliding into several of the lashed crew before grabbing the unconscious sailor. The wind whistles then roars as a wave crashes over the rail and slams into me, loosening my grip as I choke on the sea. For a moment, I am disoriented and fear we are both going overboard. Before that can happen, a fist tightens on my shirt, reminding me to regain my own grip, and drags us back as the ship rocks in the opposite direction.

"Don't you dare go overboard," Lennox calls over the wind. We grasp one another's forearms while I stand, bracing ourselves against the weather before mirroring one another's tight smiles to mask our shared fear.

After what seems an endless afternoon the storm relents, the skies clear, and each of us sighs in relief. Casting my eyes over the crew and ship I count to make sure all are present, even if each of us is ragged and exhausted from the mental and physical fatigue of weathering a storm at sea.

Lennox claps me on the back, his hair slicked back with the rain. "Well, friend, we made it through." He smiles broadly, almost as though the storm thrilled him, but I cannot do the same. Now that the waves have calmed and my duties are done, all I can think about is how Siobhan fared below deck.

"Go on," Lennox orders, jerking his chin toward the hold. "Go check on your priestess and report back. Hopefully, she handled it well. Don't tarry too long, we need to get back on course."

Soaked to the bone, but relieved that the worst is over, I stumble down the stairs to check on Siobhan.

CHAPTER 18
SIOBHAN

It only takes the ship rocking dramatically a time or two before I can't stop myself from retching into the chamber pot in our cabin. Tears flow unbidden from the fear and nausea the storm brings, and I wrap myself in one of the woolen blankets while trying to maintain some form of composure hanging onto the bunk and staring at the blackness outside the small window. The crash of waves drowns out the sound of the wind and rain, and the only light I have is the flickering lantern hanging and rocking along with the storm, casting shadows over the room.

How can they stand it on deck? What if that great funnel sweeps someone overboard? What if the hull gives way and sucks me out the side of the ship?

The thoughts come fast and each one is worse than the next. I hate being trapped in the middle of the sea without anywhere to go except the depths. If I thought I missed land before, I was mistaken. The ache for solid ground is now almost painful, fed by my fear of being lost in the storm-swollen sea.

In an attempt to smother my fear, I retreat inward, to the place I've escaped to the past years when I needed to soothe myself in the army camp. Breathing deeply, I sink to the floor and curl into a ball on our pallet, braced against the side of the bunk, trying to still my mind, even as my body is rocked violently by the wicked waves. Praying to the Goddess for the safety of the ship, I let my mind wander — to the past, to still pools, to anything other than white caps and worry and dancing shadows on the walls. Suddenly, the rocking of the boat fades and I see the crescent sigil that appeared once before, one that matches mine and my lost sisters'. This time though, an entire face appears, one that is strikingly familiar and unknown all at once.

A priestess who looks like the figurehead of the *Bartered Soul*.

Black hair hangs in a tangled mess around hollow cheeks and empty indigo eyes as the girl in my vision is swept up by a large man at the bidding of a buxom red-haired woman. The redhead looks around nervously but squares her shoulders and leads the way into a blurry building, where the man gently carries the broken priestess. I strain to make out the sign on the building, the streets, any landmarks at all, but it's no use. The vision fades as abruptly as it began, and I lay trembling on the mattress trying to calm my frayed nerves.

Shaking my head to clear my thoughts, I realize the ship, while still rocking, has steadied a bit, and I clamber to my feet to look out the window. The skies are now a lighter grey, not completely safe yet, but not the ominous black we first entered. Exhaling a breath of relief, I wait for Erik to return, taking a deep drink from the spilled pitcher to wash the taste of sickness and the tang of fear from my mouth.

I'm anxious to relay my vision to Captain Lennox. I'm certain this is the woman Lennox has been pining for. Perhaps he can deduce her location or understand the meaning. Maybe I can help him save one of my sisters after all. But I worry about what will happen if I'm wrong and the vision hasn't happened, or if something changes and it never happens at all. Is it worth getting his hopes up? It's happened before that I've upset someone with a vision for naught.

It's not long after the grip of my *Sight* relents that the cabin door swings wide and my waterlogged Northman is in my arms. As soon as he opened the door I was on my feet, throwing the blanket aside and my body against his.

"Are you all right? Was anyone hurt?" I ask, pulling back and scanning his broad frame, forgetting my fears as I examine him. The light-colored linen of his shirt is see-through from the rain, clinging to his lean muscles and showing the dark marks of his tattoos through the fabric. When I drag my eyes from the pleasant sight and up to his face, I find him smiling gently down at me, eyes sparkling from amusement and the adrenaline of surviving the storm.

"I am well, my love. No one was lost. A few injuries, but nothing we are unable to handle. You need not worry for me," he answers, and the endearment isn't lost on me. My heart skips a beat, and my stomach flips, each time he says the word *love*, even if it isn't a true declaration.

"I will always worry for you, Erik. Any time we are apart. I fear you'll have to get used to it, as I'm rather attached to you now." I mean the words to be pleasant, but my smile falters along with his at the confession. We both know we will have to be apart soon, even if neither has mentioned it.

"Siobhan, I do not wish to leave you. We should discuss this—"

"Not yet, Erik. Not now," I interrupt, placing my fingertips against his lips. "You need dry clothing and to get warm. We can talk about the future soon enough, but let's get you out of these." Ignoring the tickle of tears behind my eyes and the residual tremor of my hands, I give a sly smirk, tugging his soaked shirt from his waistband and then dragging it over his head. "Hmmm… I don't know if one of these blankets will be enough to warm you up," I tease, dragging my nails along the ridges of his stomach and across the top of his breeches. "See! Goosebumps!" I feign indignation as I towel him off with one of the blankets.

"Siobhan, there is work to do," Erik whispers, his voice ragged as I unbutton his wet breeches and struggle to pull them off while the fabric sticks to his thighs.

"*Shhh*. You might fall ill if I don't make sure you're completely dry."

He kicks off his wet boots and I grin as I kneel to tug his pants down, rubbing the blanket over his well-muscled legs. Gazing up at him from my knees I nearly laugh at his expression, he looks torn between lust and duty until I wrap my hand around him and take him into my mouth.

"Siobhan," he groans with a breathy chuckle. "Lennox will have my hide if I don't get back on deck."

Sitting back on my heels, still holding him in my grip I

reply, "Let me handle Lennox's complaints and enjoy the moment. We survived."

When I return to my task, his big hand tangles in my hair and I hear his sigh turn into a soft groan. "Whatever you say, my love."

CHAPTER 19
ERIK

I almost miss the knock at the cabin door, preoccupied as I am pressing Siobhan's soft body between myself and the wall. She clings to me as I bury my face in her hair and her moans of pleasure echo my own with each thrust. The scent of herbs on her is intoxicating and I ignore the knock too many times before Lennox's booted foot lands a kick against the wood.

"Damn it, Erik. We need you back—" Lennox pauses, his eyes glittering with surprised delight as he takes us in. I have Siobhan between me and the wall at the end of the bunk on the right side of the room, so he has a full view of my bare ass and the side of her perfect breast and thigh wrapped around my waist while I am still buried in her. "Well. Don't stop on my account, seems like your priestess is doing perfectly well. All that worry for nothing." He grins and raises his brows approvingly while Siobhan blushes furiously as she holds tight to me.

Anger threads through me as I turn to shield her, grabbing a blanket to wrap around her before I deposit her on the bed. Not caring that I am naked and still glisten from her pleasure, I whirl on Lennox, clearing the space between us in two paces before grabbing the front of his soaked shirt in one fist and slamming him against the wall. "Get the fuck out, Billy," I snarl.

"Easy, friend," Lennox soothes. "It was a joke, Erik." He holds his hands up, not returning my anger as his eyes soften. "Take a breath and take your hands off me. I didn't see anything I haven't seen before. But get your ass dressed and get back on deck, you can finish bedding her when the ship is in order." His eyes still gleam with amusement, but his tone is all quiet command. He could easily strip me of my title for laying hands on him or call for a vote of the crew to remove me. Not that he would. But still, I release him immediately, stepping back and lowering my gaze.

"Sorry."

"No need. Just get your shit together." Keeping his eyes downcast, instead of looking at her wrapped in a blanket, he adds, "Siobhan, I'm glad you're safe." With that, Lennox walks out of the room without another look, leaving the door kicked open while I scrub my hand over my face.

"That went well," she mutters, holding back a smile.

"I must return to my duties, Siobhan. I am sorry for that interruption."

More sorry than she knows.

Burying her face in her hands to hide the blush on her cheeks, she peeks above her freckled fingers with a giggle as I grab a spare pair of pants from the top of my trunk. I exhale deeply and huff an embarrassed laugh with her as I tug my pants on. Siobhan remains wrapped in a quilt perched on the edge of the other bunk watching me. The sight of her freckled legs peeking from under it is almost enough to have me back where this started, but I take a deep breath, adjust myself, and pull on my boots and a shirt. "I will be back."

"May I come up?" she asks, standing and dropping the blanket.

I groan at the sight of her nakedness but she quickly grabs a shift and dress and dons both before either of us gets any other ideas.

"I can help if anyone is injured or needs assistance," she adds shyly, pulling on her boots and scraping her fiery hair into a knot at her nape. With a smile, she raises to her tiptoes, pulling my face down to hers for a chaste kiss. "But don't think we're finished with what Lennox interrupted. I expect to pick right back up when we return," she whispers against my mouth, then nips at my lower lip with her teeth before retreating through the door, leaving me to exhale a ragged sigh and adjust myself once more before following her.

***

"Will you be leaving us then?" Lennox asks. He stands at my side scanning the crew and ship from the quarterdeck as the sun sinks below the horizon.

I drag my gaze from Siobhan as she ties a linen bandage around one of the crew member's palms where one of the ropes tore through the skin during the storm.

"What?" I question, cocking my head.

"When we land on Delosia. Should I plan on finding a new quartermaster? I'm sure Pike will step in if needed."

"Why would I be leaving you? Is this about earlier?"

Lennox barks a laugh. "No. I'm impressed that you didn't hit me if I'm being honest," he replies. "I didn't know if you'd be setting up a home with her on land is all. I knew you fancied one another, but I've never seen you this way. I wouldn't blame you if you did." Lennox places a hand on my shoulder and smiles at me, but his eyes are sad.

"We have not discussed Delosia. Or anything beyond this voyage." I swallow, looking back down toward Siobhan. She brushes stray strands of her copper waves from her eyes, but the wind blows them right back as she smiles up at us.

"You should, Erik. If you feel the way I think you do, you should." With that, Lennox pats my shoulder once more, then descends the stairs toward his cabin. I follow behind a few moments later, meeting Siobhan in the center of the deck.

"Are you free to enjoy your evening now, Quartermaster?" Siobhan asks, but her teasing tone is muted as she scans the darkening water and surveys the clouds in the twilight sky.

"I am. Are you well?"

"I'm fine. I just hope we don't experience anything like that storm again. I fear I might die of fright if we do." She shivers, wrapping her arms around herself as the wind picks up. "I confess, I lied earlier when you came to check on me. It shook me more than I cared to admit. How much longer until we are on solid ground again?"

Sighing inwardly at the knowledge that solid ground means we will likely be parted, I reply, "A week until

Delosia, maybe less with good winds. I promise the beauty of the island will make up for the storm."

"Well, then it's up to you to make up for it in the meantime." When I glance down at her I find her eyes hooded, she bites her lower lip delicately before running her fingers down my forearm and distracting me from the conversation Lennox encouraged me to begin.

CHAPTER 20
SIOBHAN

Lying awake in the silence of our cabin, I focus on Erik's breathing and the creak of the ship. If I dwell on the fact that we're only a few days from land I might blurt out that I love him, but that I can't possibly travel by ship again anytime soon. The storm was terrifying, even if I continue to try to mask the distress it caused me. Before the storm, I was able to ignore the subtle changes in the weather, even if the idea that only a few planks of wood separated us from an endless ocean was daunting. Now, each time the winds pick up, or the sails crack, I feel panic clawing at my throat with nowhere to escape to but the depths themselves.

Erik has something on his mind too, but the two of us have been tiptoeing around the inevitable, smothering it in kisses and caresses. I'll ask him his plans once my feet are on land. I can talk to Lennox then too, before they have to set sail again. I still haven't told him about my vision of his priestess. I shouldn't be embarrassed that he walked in on Erik and me, especially since I saw sadness flash in his eyes briefly when I peeked over Erik's shoulder, not lust. I'm certain his longing is not because he desires either of us, but because of his own loneliness and need. The desperation in his eyes when he questioned me was obvious, perhaps I can offer some consolation to him in repayment for bringing me to safety. I only hope it proves to be an accurate vision.

The water has become breathtakingly clear in the past few days, offering some relief from the fear of being lost in the waves. I've spent as much time as I can above deck, perched near the railing and staring into the depths. The waves lull me into an almost dreamlike-state and I've *Seen* the dark-haired priestess another time or two, but those same waves have also brought me visions of darkness and blood, and their crash against the hull mimics the howls of animals at times, sending gooseflesh rippling over me. I write down what I *See* when I'm able, but nothing makes sense to me. Not yet at least.

Curling on my side I admire Erik's dark outline in the shadows of the room. He sleeps peacefully, and I envy him his rest. I fear mine will be hard-won until I know for certain what my future holds.

THE BEACH OF DELOSIA IS UNLIKE ANY I SAW BACK HOME IN Selennia. The white sand glitters in the sun as though diamonds are scattered through it, like the shimmering white stone of our temples, and it nearly blinds me when I scan the shoreline. Erik leaves me on the dock so he can assist in directing the crew on orders from Lennox. Rather than staying with the crates, I find myself on the beach, my skirts gathered above my knees and boots discarded so I can wade into the crystal sea. I lose track of time admiring sea stars undulating and tiny crabs scurrying in the tides until a shadow falls across the sand where I've sat above the tideline. When I glance up, Erik smiles down at me, and the happiness in his eyes fills my chest with as much light as the bright sun overhead so that I beam a smile back.

"I can escort you to your lodging if you're ready, my love." Erik offers a hand to help me stand and we retrieve my boots before taking a winding path through the thick jungle beyond the beach. He chuckles when I stop every few feet to admire the plants of Delosia — the bright colors of the flowers, the sweet smell of the fruit, and the lush greenery of the forest pulling my attention every direction along the pathway.

Stopping near the center of town, Erik points to a two-story building. "You can stay here; Lennox has an arrangement with the owner and they always keep extra rooms open for him." Erik pushes the door open to reveal the open-air courtyard of a boarding house full of patrons cheerfully eating and drinking in the dappled light of an early afternoon.

"And where will you stay?" I ask, suddenly worried he has an arrangement elsewhere.

"Where would you like me to stay?"

"With me..." *Always*, I almost add, but bite my tongue, giving him a sideways smile instead.

"Siobhan, we must speak about things," Erik begins, but one of the serving girls approaches us, interrupting him.

"Hello, Erik!" The young woman smiles, her dark skin is luminous in the island sun streaming overhead as she inspects me. "Have you and Lennox brought us another friend this trip?" she asks, with a welcoming smile.

"Giselle, this is Siobhan," Erik says. "She will need lodging."

"All right, for how long?" Giselle asks, smiling at me in turn.

Erik rubs his hand across the back of his neck, cutting his eyes toward me with a pause. "That is to be seen."

Giselle's brows raise, but she doesn't ask questions. "Very well, she can have one of the downstairs rooms. I'll get the key from Alvaro and make sure the room is ready. Grab a table, I'll bring you drinks." With a swish of bright-colored skirts, Giselle has turned and retreated to the bar, dropping her tray and disappearing into the back of the courtyard.

Erik and I sit in silence, sipping the cool, fruity, rum-filled drink that Giselle dropped off on her way to check my room. My eyes drift over the space, taking in the huge potted plants and trees throughout the courtyard. The island breeze makes the humid heat more bearable, but I still have to pull the damp fabric of my dress away from my heated skin in the unfamiliar climate.

"It's so much warmer here than I expected," I finally say.

"It is. I always miss home more than ever when I am here. I miss the icy waters and cutting wind. But I do enjoy Delosia. It is hospitable to our crew and any guests we bring. Lennox has family of a sort here, so we stop on the island frequently in our travels." He looks at me then, longing in his eyes and my heartbeat speeds up.

"Your room is ready, mistress," Giselle interrupts,

placing a brass key on the table next to me along with two more drinks for us. "Only one key, so the two of you will just have to share it."

"Oh, I will not—"

"Thank you, Giselle," I interrupt Erik's protests. "We can make that arrangement work just fine." Heat blooms in my cheeks and slithers down to my core when I meet Erik's eyes.

"I thought it might," Giselle remarks with a laugh, then retreats to her work, leaving us staring at one another.

"I did not wish to impose upon you," Erik mutters, drinking the rest of his drink and taking the new cup.

"We've shared quarters for weeks, why would now be any different?"

"I did not want you to think you were bound to me just because we shared a bed on the ship. This is why we need to speak. I cannot offer you the life you deserve, Siobhan."

"Erik," I begin, but he's staring into his cup. "Erik Varangr. Look at me." My tone grabs his attention, even if my words are clumsy from the strong drink, and his blue eyes narrow on me as I continue to speak. "I have not shared your cabin, your bed, or your body these past few weeks because I felt obligated to, or just because I find you physically appealing. I told you the night of the full moon, you feel like home to me."

I take a deep breath, this was not the way I thought this conversation would go — in the middle of a public court-yard slightly drunk on fruit juice and rum — but my courage is screwed up as tight as I think it will ever be, so I blurt, "I love you, Erik. No matter what life you think I deserve, I only want one with you in it. Whatever that may look like."

Erik's eyes take on a glassy appearance as my words sink in. I grip the new cup and take a deep swallow, hoping that the rum will help mask my nervousness as I wait for his response.

"I love you too, Siobhan."

"What?" I gasp, my head swimming from the rum.

"I love you. I have wanted to tell you, but the time never felt right. I did not wish to cage you in or ask for you to commit to a man who has no solid ground to call home. I know you hate living on the ship, you need a place that is safe and secure. I did not know if that was something I could provide for you." Erik swallows and reaches across the table to take my hand in his. "I promise I will keep you safe. I will be home for you if that is how you feel."

Grabbing the key from the table with my left hand, I cling to Erik's with my right, standing and pulling him to his feet. "Which room is ours?"

CHAPTER 21
ERIK

Siobhan drags me down the hallway on the left side of the courtyard, her gait only mildly impaired by the spiked pineapple juice Giselle provided. My heart pounds and my chest is light from our mutual confession.

She loves me. But how can I possibly keep her?

As she bends to insert the key into the lock of the door, I ignore the ache I feel when I think of leaving her behind. Instead, I focus on the soft warmth of her body as I wrap my hands around her waist, pressing against her backside and groaning when she pushes back into my groin with a giggle. As soon as the door swings open, I spin her in my arms, lifting her off her feet and carrying her into the room, our mouths crashing together as she drops the key to the floor with a metallic *clink*.

Kicking the door shut behind me, I moan against her lips. She tastes sweet and spiced like our drinks, but her taste and scent are there too, intoxicating me further as I grip beneath her thighs. She caresses my cheeks with her delicate hands as our tongues dance, letting little whimpers of pleasure free when I grind against her.

"Erik." My name on Siobhan's lips is a prayer I'll never tire of hearing.

Pulling away from her, the sight of her bright eyes and flushed skin ignites my desire further, and I look around to inspect the room. The bed waits to the right of where we stand, so I carry Siobhan to it and lay her across its light-weight, blue and yellow, floral quilt. She sits up, propped on her elbows grinning at me as I stand over her, dragging her gaze down my body until it settles on my cock straining against the front of my breeches.

With her lower lip between her teeth, Siobhan sits forward, reaching for my belt when I catch her wrists in one hand. A little gasp escapes her at my sudden motion, but when I pin her arms over her head she sighs and writhes against me, pressing herself against my length with a breathy groan.

"Let me take my time, Siobhan. We have nowhere else to be, no one to come knocking, no other duties to tend to tonight. Let me love you the way you deserve." I release my grip on her wrists, running my hand down her arms, the column of her throat, over her breasts, and to her waist while my lips trail down her neck.

"Yes," she breathes, pulling my mouth to hers for a moment before I kneel on the floor and run my hands up her smooth calves, then the outside of her thighs, rucking her skirts up to bare her to me. She gasps as I kiss up her inner thigh, nipping and tasting her freckled skin the entire way. When my mouth settles over the apex of her thighs, tongue and fingers slipping between the wet heat I find there, she arches into me, gripping my braid and grinding herself into me. Her moans become louder as her movements become erratic, making me painfully hard as her pleasure crashes over her and her muscles pulse around my fingers. Her arousal slicks my beard, but I relish it as she shudders and pants, riding the wave of her release.

Exhaling a breathy chuckle, Siobhan releases her fingers from my hair and gazes down at me with hooded eyes. The flush on her cheeks is beautiful, and my pride swells knowing I am responsible for her satisfaction. But I am not finished pleasing her. Standing, I pull my shirt over my head, then kick out of my boots, unfastening my belt as they *thunk* against the wall.

Siobhan sits up, unfastening the clasps of her bodice quickly and pushing it off her shoulders until she is left in just her shift. I lean over her, capturing her lips as I palm her breast through the thin fabric, then unlace the front and push the shoulders off, pulling both her dress and shift off and tossing them on the floor in a heap.

I pause to admire the swell of her breasts, the dip of her waist, and the flare of her hips illuminated by the island sun slanting through the shuttered window. Under my gaze she scoots back farther on the soft bed, squeezing her thighs together and blushing more thoroughly, filling my heart with love for her gentle beauty.

"Take off your pants and have me however you'd like, my love," she whispers, her brogue rough in the quiet room. My heart clenches at the endearment. "Like you said, there shouldn't be any interruptions tonight."

When I snap my gaze to her, she smiles sweetly, but runs her fingers over her collarbone, through loose strands of her wavy red hair, and down over her breasts, all while opening her knees to give me a full view between her thighs.

As I watch, her hand continues its exploration down her belly and she slides her fingers through her center. It's all I can do to not rip my pants from my body, but I calmly push them off before settling between her thighs. I want to do as I said, to take my time, but my need for her is almost painful as we kiss and tease one another, sliding my length against her slick core. Her sounds of pleasure are almost my undoing, but I hold myself back, trailing my tongue over her peaked nipple and sucking it into my mouth as she arches into me. Muscles trembling, I hold myself away from her, but she pulls me closer tilting her hips to meet mine.

"Erik, please," she moans. I position myself at her entrance and ease myself into her, sucking in a gasp at the feel of her wrapping around me. When I'm fully seated, Siobhan wraps her legs around my back, pulling me closer with each thrust. "More, Erik. *Harder*."

I've held back before, even in the aftermath of the storm when I had her against the wall. But now, with her begging, I raise up on one hand, gripping her wrists in the other to hold above her head.

"Tell me if you want me to stop, Siobhan. I don't want to hurt you," I murmur against the shell of her ear and feel her shiver under me as her breasts press against my chest.

"You won't," she replies as she tightens her legs around me.

So, I do as she asks.

I take her harder, wringing deep moans from her as I pick up a punishing pace while gripping her slim wrists over her head. She cries out my name as I feel her clench around me with her second release. Then I chase my own.

As I loosen my hold on her wrists, prepared to pull out before I come, she grips my shoulders and pulls me closer with her legs still wrapped around my hips.

"Don't." She rolls her hips against me. "It's the wrong moon phase for me to get with child, you needn't worry."

For a moment, I'm torn, but she pulls me to her, kissing me fiercely and I once again, do as she asks.

CHAPTER 22
SIOBHAN

I'm sore in the most pleasant ways when I wake the next morning. The light of the sunrise casts a warm glow over the room. The soft linens shift, baring my back as I arch in a stretch. Erik still lays at my side and a satisfied rumble greets me as he reaches over to affectionately squeeze my backside when I arch further. I exhale a small laugh as I slide back down onto my belly, smiling at him. His hair came loose from its usual braid at some point in the night and the dark brown strands lay loose over his shoulders. Running his fingers over the ink on my back, I can tell he's tracing the lines of the runic markings I wear.

Rolling over, I wrap my leg over his and kiss him deeply, before pulling back to say, "I need Lennox."

Erik's hand stills and he cants his head before answering. "After the night we had I did not expect you to ask for my captain this morning."

Huffing another soft laugh, I lay back shaking my head. "I don't need him in any of the ways I needed you last night, don't fret. But I had a vision, several now, that I think will interest him. Or at least that might soothe his heart."

"Of what?"

"I believe it's the priestess he seeks. I can't be certain of course, but she looks similar to the description and the figurehead."

"This is news he will want to hear, whether it leads him to her or not. I do not know all the details of his attachment to the woman, but he has sought her since I met him." Erik pulls me close, wrapping his arms around me and tucking me under his chin so my back meets his chest, and whispers, "If you didn't see her on this island, though, can it wait until breakfast?"

Heat blooms in my chest and spreads to my core at his suggestive whisper and comforting embrace. Even if I was slightly drunk last night, all the alcohol did was boost my confidence in telling him how I felt and the memory of him returning my declaration of love nearly brings tears to my eyes. We've only known one another for six weeks, but I'm certain I've found my future in this man. As he nuzzles my neck my joy dims, remembering that we may only have a short time together before he sails again, but we can discuss that soon enough.

WHEN WE EMERGE FROM OUR ROOM AND ENTER THE courtyard it's mid-morning and Giselle greets us with a wide, knowing smile.

"Good morning," the young woman says, eyes twinkling. "Can I bring anything from the kitchen?"

Erik nods and we take a table while Giselle disappears to retrieve our late breakfast. While we wait, I admire the bright flowers in one of the pots vining up the trunk of a small fruit tree. Movement on the upper balcony overlooking the courtyard draws my eye, so I catch sight of Lennox striding from what I assume is his room before descending the stairs. Erik hails him so he takes the seat next to me.

Lennox is more casual here than when I first saw him in Selennia. No longer is he swathed in his heavy greatcoat. Instead, he's traded it for a simple linen shirt with the sleeves cuffed to show his tanned and tattooed forearms. His skin has a golden tan from the voyage and his fair hair gleams in the sunlight streaming through the open ceiling of the courtyard. He's relaxed and calm as I inspect him from the corner of my eye. I almost feel bad knowing that my vision might interfere with his peace.

"Good morning," Lennox says as he leans back in his seat, motioning for Giselle to bring him a cup to share our pot of tea, then adds with a smirk, "I hope the two of you found your lodgings comfortable."

My cheeks heat, but I simply smile in return. "Good morning."

"Siobhan has news," Erik advises and any idea I might have had about waiting to tell Lennox fades.

"Is that so?" Lennox eyes me curiously. "I have some for her as well."

His reply surprises me, my heart lurching momentarily, though I don't know why. "How is it that you'd have news for me, Captain?"

"I spoke with an old friend at dinner last night. She has

a high standing here on Delosia and is a well-respected leader, but she lived in Selennia for some time before Blackwell's arrival. I told her about you and she may have a position for you, should you want it." Lennox takes a moment to pour his tea now that Giselle passed by with a cup but he looks between Erik and me expectantly. When the silence stretches on, he exhales loudly and takes a sip of the steaming tea. "Don't tell me you two still haven't discussed your arrangements."

"We… well, we…" I begin while Erik starts, "We were otherwise occupied." Both of us stop speaking and smile across the table, trying to keep from laughing.

Lennox chuckles, taking another sip of tea. "I should have known. Siobhan, Marie would like to meet you this afternoon to discuss what she had in mind for you, if you're interested. Erik, I need you on the dock to direct the crew and determine if Pike needs you for anything. Go after breakfast, before you two get tangled in the sheets and go missing for the rest of the day again."

"I don't know where to go." I look nervously at Erik, the idea of wandering the streets alone a daunting prospect. I still haven't fully explained what's in my heart, but now nerves have taken hold at the thought of making permanent plans here on this strange island, coloring the reality of my choices much starker in the morning light.

"I'll take you. Marie was close with my family. Very close, in fact. I told her I would bring you by since I knew Erik would be busy." Grabbing a slice of toast and downing the remainder of his tea, Lennox stands. "I'll meet you out front at two o'clock." As he turns to leave, he whirls back around. "You said you had news for me?"

"I'll tell you on our walk, if that suits you, Captain?"

"William."

"William," I amend with a soft smile at his insistence.

"Tell your woman goodbye for the day, Erik. I'll meet you out front in fifteen minutes." With that, he places his tricorne hat atop his blond hair and strides through the tables toward the front door.

"You will like Marie. She is a kind woman. It is good that she may have something for you," Erik murmurs, but his jaw is tight and his eyes scan my face for a sign of what I'm thinking.

"Yes. It's nice of him to speak with her for me." My words are agreeable, but my stomach knots as our situation presses down on me. Erik and I may love each other, we may have finally admitted it out loud last night, even if our bodies had already confirmed it weeks ago, but my head reminds my heart that it won't be long before reality may come between us.

CHAPTER 23
SIOBHAN

I wash and tidy myself as best as I can in the basin in our room before meeting Lennox in the sunny street at two o'clock. I'll need to purchase new clothing soon, and the fact that the dress I've been wearing was designed for Selennia's cool climate is glaringly obvious as I begin to sweat in the humid heat of Delosia. I look back longingly at the loose linen of Giselle's bright ensemble where she tidies the courtyard, wishing the wool of my dress breathed as nicely as hers surely does. Pushing a stray strand of hair from my eyes, I smile at Lennox in greeting, no longer fearful of his wild eyes or sarcastic grin.

"You look lovely, Siobhan," Lennox says, holding his arm out for me to take so he can guide me through the sandy streets of the town. "But I'll be sure to take you by the seamstress after our errand, she can help you get something more comfortable."

"That's thoughtful of you, William. Thank you." I'm surprised that he would think of such things, but appreciate it nonetheless. "Wouldn't it be better for me to do so after

I've earned something, though? I wouldn't want to impose any more than I already have on your hospitality."

"Nonsense. You helped patch my crew up on the voyage, you deserve fair pay just like the rest of the crew." He strolls slowly while I cast my gaze over the bright buildings and plants. The silence stretches for a bit before he mutters more softly, as though he shouldn't say the words, "Would you consider continuing to sail with us in such a fashion? As the ship's surgeon? Or are you determined to stay on land?"

I can't hide the surprise on my face as my mouth pops open. "Oh, I hadn't considered that option."

"It would make Erik happy, and if it would make you happy, you'd be welcome and safe with us. I don't want to meddle more than I already have in your affairs, but I wanted you to know the offer stands, directly from me, should Erik tell you about it later." Lennox's expression is soft, reminiscent of the way he looked the night of the full moon when he accepted my comfort for his sadness, reminding me that I need to tell him of my vision.

"I'll think about it. Though, I confess, I did not find the seafaring life to be a pleasant one. But I thank you. I'll speak with Erik about it this evening. Now, there's something I must tell you."

Halting, I tug his arm until he joins me under one of the awnings of a corner shop. The shade is cool and a breeze blows in from the direction of the beach making the damp cloth of my dress feel refreshing instead of stifling. If the heat is always like this I just might reconsider getting back on the ship.

"Yes, you mentioned news. What is it?" Lennox stands

a few paces away, crossing his arms over his chest as he leans against the side of the building. The light sheen of sweat on his brow doesn't seem to trouble him the way it does me, but his eyes are piercing as he waits for me to speak.

"It may seem strange, but I've had a vision. One that's recurred a few times now since meeting you. Mind you, what I *See* doesn't always mean that the events have, or will, happen, but I thought you needed to hear." I stumble over my words, trying to explain so he doesn't get his hopes up.

"Go on." His brows raise in curiosity.

"Do you know a red-haired woman? She's lovely, well-dressed, and quite shapely. Lives in a city perhaps?"

"My sister. Celeste. It must be her. Was she with a child?" Lennox pushes off the wall and steps closer, leaning over me with a gleam of panic edging his eyes. "Has something happened to them?"

"No, nothing like that. It's just that I believe the priestess you seek is either with her or will be soon. In the vision, I *See* a dark-haired woman on her knees in front of your sister, almost as if she's begging. A big, dark-skinned man picks her up and they retreat into a building, but I saw the barest glimpse of a sigil and sad blue eyes."

I study his face for a moment and find warring emotions. His eyes drift down the street in the direction we were heading before I pulled us into the shade, then toward the docks as though debating if he can run to his ship immediately.

"William," I start, tugging on his sleeve to grab his attention once more. "I can't promise it's true, but I wanted you to know. Does your sister still live in Selennia? Would she take in a priestess knowing what could happen?"

"Yes." Lennox's voice is a ragged whisper. His hands shake as he removes his tricornered hat and runs his fingers through his hair. "She's a madame in Artemisia. I haven't visited her since I took my own ship, but I'm certain it's her. The man you described is one of her guards, Jacob. And yes, she would take her in. She knows I've been looking for a woman with that description, but she would protect any priestess in honor of our mother. Thank you, Siobhan. Thank you for telling me and giving me hope."

With a deep breath, he stops fidgeting with his hat and replaces it, looking once more toward the docks as though he's fighting an internal battle to stay where he is. Then, he straightens his shoulders and offers his arm once more. "Now, let's see if I can offer you some as well."

THE VISIT WITH MARIE TAKES LONGER THAN I ANTICIPATED. She's a lovely older woman who greets Lennox with a warm hug and me with a kind smile. Lennox accepts a pour of whiskey, but downs it quickly, then excuses himself from the house.

"I'll be back. I just need some air," he says before escaping through the front door and leaving me in Marie's company.

"The apothecary is an old man, older than I am even," Marie explains once we are settled in her parlor, her dark skin crinkling with a laugh. Despite her comment, she appears ageless except for a few fine lines and her silver hair which she wears braided tight to her scalp and wrapped in a bright cloth. "He needs someone young who can help tend to his business and work in his garden outside of town. He has a spare room upstairs and is an honest and sweet man. You could live there comfortably, and it sounds like you have the knowledge needed to assist him. It would be a perfect option for both of you should you decide to stay here."

"I would like to meet him, to see what it is he would need and what the shop and garden look like. I still have to discuss my plans, but it sounds lovely." I sip my tea and smile, but tears burn behind my eyes. It *does* sound lovely, but my heart aches at the thought of saying goodbye to Erik and staying on this strange island on my own.

"We can arrange that for tomorrow if you'd like, early in the morning to avoid the hottest time," Marie says, taking a few notes. "Would that give you some time to speak with William's quartermaster?" When she sees my eyes grow wide, she adds, "William already told me of your situation. You wouldn't be the first woman who has to figure out her life alone while her man is at sea. My brother was a sailor, and so was my son."

"Oh, I see." My eyes blur a bit with the tears I continue to hold in, forcing me to blink a few times to clear them. "Yes. Yes, I think tomorrow morning would work fine. Thank you, Mistress Marie. I'll speak with Erik tonight."

The walk back to the boarding house is quiet, both Lennox and I are lost in our thoughts, even forgetting our original plan to visit the seamstress' shop. I'm glad of the oversight though, I'm no longer in the right mood to look at fabrics or to consider fashion now. When Lennox bids me farewell in the courtyard, I watch him settle onto a stool at the bar with a glass of whiskey before I retreat to my room.

Erik waits at the small table when I enter our quarters with a bottle of wine and a nervous expression. "How was your meeting with Mistress Marie?"

Approaching him, I wrap my arms around his shoulders and sit on his lap. He returns the gesture by wrapping his arms around my waist to hold me close. "She was kind."

He nuzzles his nose against my neck before placing a tender kiss on my pulse, sending a shiver over me. "And?"

"And I think we must speak plainly about what the future holds for us," I sigh. I sit back a bit so we can look at one another. I can only assume my face mimics his — full of love and anguish at our options.

CHAPTER 24
ERIK

"Erik," Siobhan begins, her voice soft and hesitant. "What do you want from this? From us?"

I knew we needed to have this discussion. I should have spoken with her about it before we docked and before she met with Marie, but I wasn't ready to put into words the fact that we might part. The idea of leaving her shreds my heart, but the loss of being part of Lennox's crew, a life I've come to love, is just as painful. It would be selfish to ask her to come, not only because of the danger she would face at sea, but because she was miserable and afraid most of the voyage here. How could I ask her to do that for months on end with no home to come to?

"I want *you*, Siobhan. I want to ask you to come with me. To sail with us, to see the world. To show you the dancing night skies of the Northern Isles. But I think I already know your answer to that," I confess keeping my eyes focused on my hand twirling a strand of copper curls between my fingers. Meeting her eyes, I add, "I love you, but I cannot ask you to risk yourself at sea for me alone. If you want to come with us, you will be more than welcome, but I do not think that is what your heart wants. Or what your soul needs."

Tears well in her blue eyes, making them burn brighter in the lantern light. "I love you, Erik. From the moment I first saw you I knew you were special and that we were meant to meet. I wish I could come with you. I *want* to be with you. I want you to stay with me. But just as you said, your soul would not be content to be trapped on this tropical island. You said it yourself that you miss the cold waters of the Northern Isles. As much as you may love me, this isn't where your final home should be."

Tears begin to fall, trailing over her freckled cheeks as she forces a smile and dashes them from her pretty face. My own tears escape in solidarity, drifting into my beard as we press our foreheads together.

"But this isn't our end, Erik. Just because I can't sail with you and you can't stay with me, doesn't mean this is our end. You and Lennox return here frequently. I have no plans to leave. Each time you come back I'll be here waiting for you. This is not the end for us, you just have to come back to me." Her voice is choked with emotion, and a little sob escapes before she buries her face in the fabric of my shirt and her shoulders shake with her tears. "We *will* have a home together one day. Just not yet."

I hold her close, my sorrow matching hers even though I know our decisions are the right ones. Neither of us expected to find the other, but now we will both have something to look forward to as the days drag on. "Yes, Siobhan. We will have a home together one day. I promise you, my love."

"Somewhere I won't sweat so much, preferably," she mumbles, then hiccups a little laugh through her tears. When she sits up her cheeks are flushed and salty droplets still linger on her lashes, but she smiles broadly and kisses me deeply. "And if it turns out one of us can't bear it, the next time you come back we can discuss it again."

"Then it is settled. I will make sure the arrangements are comfortable for you before we leave, and I will return to you as often as I am able. I will always come back to you, Siobhan."

I stroke my thumb over her cheeks, drying her tears and forcing mine back down. It seems that Lennox won't be the only one pining over a woman on the *Bartered Soul* from now on.

CHAPTER 25
SIOBHAN

In the two weeks since arriving on Delosia and meeting Marie, I've come to enjoy the little island. Even the humid heat is growing on me. The morning after Erik and I made our decisions, I met the gentle Mister Simons, the elderly man who owns the apothecary, and immediately knew I'd made the correct choice.

While my heart yearns to be with Erik, the overflowing garden and comfortable apothecary shop with a private apartment above it are something I could only have dreamed of a few months ago when I was still trapped in the army camp. It offers the comfort and stability I've craved during the years since the temple fell, and that knowledge soothes the tightness that bands around my chest this morning.

I awoke early in the soft featherbed of the boarding house tangled with Erik for the last time for the foreseeable future. His large frame makes the bed a tight fit, but with our days together waning I haven't cared about the lack of space each night as I curl next to him. Soon enough I'll have the room above the apothecary to myself and I know I'll miss his warmth and scent surrounding me. We dined together in our room, avoiding the other sailors who were preparing for the voyage in the courtyard, and soaked up our last hours together before slipping out the front door and down the gritty streets toward the docks hand in hand.

The sun crests over the horizon, illuminating the docks already swarming with sailors with a rosy glow, and I watch as Lennox and Erik converse, then shout orders to the crew loading the *Bartered Soul*. In less time than I'd like, most of the cargo is stored and the crew makes their way onto the ship. As the final stores are loaded, I'm surprised to find Marie standing at my side.

"Good morning, Siobhan," she greets me warmly.

"Good morning, Mistress Marie," I return with a tight smile, trying to hide my emotions and keep up a pleasant façade for the kind woman. "I didn't expect you to be here today."

"I always make sure to bid William farewell and to send a little something back to Celeste and my darling Lyra." When I furrow my brow in confusion, she shows me a doll wearing colorful linen just like the women on the island favor. "Lyra's my granddaughter, William's niece." The threads of information begin to knot together as Marie leaves my side to speak with Lennox and wrap him in an embrace. He smiles at the doll and dutifully tucks it under his arm as she speaks.

Erik says a few words to Marie, too far out of earshot for me to hear, then locks eyes with me. A few long strides later he has me held to his chest. I've been fighting tears all morning and struggle to keep them at bay now, breathing in his scent and clinging to him as though he's a raft keeping me afloat. For a brief moment, I hesitate, almost blurting, "Take me with you!"

But that would be folly. No part, other than my heart, wishes to be on that ship again anytime soon. Instead, I drag Erik's mouth to mine, kissing him deeply as though he's the air I breathe. We hold one another close for another few moments before the tap of boots pulls us from each other. Lennox stands at Erik's side, still holding the doll for his niece and smiling broadly.

"I wanted to bid you farewell, Siobhan. I hope you enjoy island life. I'll make sure we bring your man back to you," Lennox says.

"Thank you for everything. And William," I call out, halting his steps as he turns to board the ship. "I brought this for you." I hold out one of the bags of herbs from the apothecary shop, pressing it into his hands. Tucking the doll under his arm once more, he opens the bag, but looks at me, then Erik, in confusion at the contents.

"I thought you might make use of them, in case you weren't quite ready for your priestess to know who you were, or if you're ever in need of subterfuge. It's something I've *Seen*," I explain as he closes the bag of black walnut hulls and shoves them in his pocket. "It won't smell very good, but if you boil them and apply the mixture to your hair, it will mask the golden color for a while."

With a smirk and a dip of his chin, Lennox tips the front of his tricorne and heads up the gangway.

"Stay safe, Erik. Return to me soon," I murmur, holding his bearded cheeks between my hands.

"I always will, my love. I promise."

With a tight embrace and a farewell kiss that makes my knees weak, Erik reluctantly releases me, our fingers clinging to one another for as long as they can before he has to fully turn to board the ship. With deep breaths I manage to push my tears down as I wave and descend to the shore next to the docks, watching the sails unfurl as the *Bartered Soul* heads toward deeper waters. When I can no longer make out Erik's expression, I sit on the white sand and let out a sob, my body shuddering with grief at his departure.

This is what I wanted, what I asked of him, and yet my heart aches from the distance already.

A soft hand pats my shoulder, turning my attention to Marie who now sits at my side. "It never really gets easier, but you'll be safe here, Siobhan. You can make a home and they *will* be back."

With a deep breath, I quiet my tears, answering on an exhale, "I know they will. I know something is coming, something important that brought us all together, Marie. I know this isn't our end."

EPILOGUE
LENNOX

One Year Later
Artemisia, Selennia

Stepping through the door of the House of Starlight I'm met with a firm hand on my shoulder halting my steps. I bristle at the familiarity, turning quickly to glare at Jacob.

"Oh! Lennox?" Jacob starts. "Is that *you*?"

"Evening, Jacob. Is the Madame in the salon?" I shrug off his touch, straightening my coat and running my fingers through my now dark brown hair. The stink of the black walnut hull mixture has finally faded, leaving me nearly unrecognizable from the last time I was on shore in my homeland. I heeded Siobhan's advice to use them, as my notoriety changes it might serve me well to change physically with it.

"She is, Captain. You know the way."

I leave Jacob at the door with a curt nod as I walk through the hallway to the main salon. I haven't seen my sister or her establishment since before Erik and I found Siobhan hiding in an alley farther south in Athene. My pulse quickens thinking about the gentle priestess we left behind on Delosia, wondering if Siobhan's vision might have come true. Could the woman I've been looking for all this time be here *now*?

Slipping through the entryway of the salon I scan the starry room, my eyes immediately landing on my sister — Madame Celeste. Her bright red hair draws the eye instantly, as does her shimmering dress, just as she wishes. She plays her role well, deftly removing the least desirables from the brothel without raising any curiosity about her, or her business, from Blackwell's patrols. I applaud her, even if I hate that she's here at all.

I take a seat in the back booth, the one she reserves for me when I'm at port. The little marker is here tonight, so she received word from my messenger that I would be in. Seeing me seated, she makes her way through the tables, smiling brightly at her customers as she glides over. I keep my head down, so she can't see my face in the candle flame yet.

"Excuse me, sir, this table is reserved tonight," Celeste advises firmly. If I were an errant customer I wouldn't hesitate to listen, but instead, I simply smile.

"Giving my table away already, Celeste?"

Her little gasp lifts my smile more broadly, and I finally look up from the candle so she can see me clearly in the light of the flame.

"Is that you? What have you done to your hair?" Celeste whispers, not wanting our conversation to be overheard. No one here knows we're related; we keep up a ruse about our business relationship to protect her and her girls.

"Nothing different than you do." I cut my eyes at her red hair, which is naturally the same golden blond as my own. "It's a wonder what a change can make in the impression one has on the rabble. Do you have any new girls? One that might interest me?" I ask the same question every time. But this time my hope is nearly painful and my heart pounds erratically.

"Actually," Celeste starts, but pauses biting her lip with indecision. "She's here. I'm almost certain it's her."

"Where?" I move to stand, looking around the room when I see her. A wraith of a woman at the end of the bar.

"Lennox, no," Celeste grabs my arm, pulling me back into my seat and attracting more attention than either of us wants.

The woman turns along with a few others. Her hair is long and black, her skin as pale as the starlight the brothel is named for, but her cheeks are hollow, her eyes vacant. An upturned crescent moon sigil, like Siobhan's and any other former priestess, is a dull scar visible on her brow. Our eyes meet for a moment before her gaze shutters and she retreats toward the foyer and stairs beyond.

"What are you doing, Celeste? Let me go to her," I plead. Doesn't she understand? I've been waiting to make sure this woman is all right, why won't she allow me to even ask her name? To offer her comfort?

"It may be her, but she's changed from whatever you think she was. She's only just begun to come downstairs since we found her. She barely speaks to anyone; it took months before she even spoke to me. She's safe here, but she will *not* welcome you. Not yet at least. You must give her time before you consider approaching her." Celeste strokes her hand on my forearm and to anyone else, it would look like she's flirting, but her eyes soften to show me she understands what I'm feeling.

"At least tell me her name?"

"She never told me. Here she goes by Andromeda."

Afterword

Thank you so much for reading Erik and Siobhan's story.

If you enjoyed this book or any of the others in the *Andromeda's Account* series, please consider leaving a review on Amazon or Goodreads (or any of your other favorite review spots).

Reviews and word of mouth are the best ways you can support your favorite indie authors, and I appreciate every review! The more people who read my stories, the more I can continue to write and share them with the world!

xo,
LB

ACKNOWLEDGMENTS

Here we are again, with another chapter in the world of *Andromeda's Account* behind us!

Thank you so much to my husband and daughter for putting up with my hyper-fixation while writing these stories and for being patient with me during editing. I love you both!

To my alphas — Krystal, Kristen, Lauren, Rhiannon, and Kelly — y'all helped me feel confident sharing this sweet novella with the world.

And Kelly, you've been such a kind and enthusiastic editor, and a wonderful friend. I appreciate you and your work so much.

To all the readers who love this world and these characters — thank you for believing in me and my storytelling, and for falling in love with my characters. Your recommendations and kind messages really make the tough days easier.

I can't wait to share what comes next with you.

About the Author

L.B. Benson is a native Texan and a lifelong reader. She formally immortalized her love of books by earning a Bachelor of Arts in English from the University of Texas. While she primarily writes romance, you can find her engrossed in almost any genre.

L.B. spends her spare time dreaming up stories in the Texas countryside where she lives with her family.

Stay up to date by following along at https://lbtheauthor.com or on social media (@lb_the_author).

instagram.com/lb_the_author